D0727834

It was as if he knew what was on her mind

"As long as we're being perfectly candid," Josh began, "why don't you tell me what Selena told you that set you against me?"

"I already told you—she insinuated that the two of you were going to get married again," Jamie hedged, too unsure of herself to mention the woman's other accusations.

"She said something else that's bred a strong thread of distrust in you."

"She mentioned your Pygmalion complex."

"My what!"

"Pygmalion complex," Jamie repeated, her voice barely above a whisper. "And you were demanding some very drastic alterations in my life."

"True. But I wasn't doing it for any personal pleasure. Can you believe that?" There was an urgency in his tone.

"I want to." She bit her lip as she glanced toward him.

Books by Betsy Page

HARLEQUIN ROMANCE
2627—THE BONDED HEART
2704—DARK-NIGHT ENCOUNTER

These books may be available at your local bookseller.

Don't miss any of our special offers. Write to us at the
following address for information on our newest releases.

Harlequin Reader Service
P.O. Box 52040, Phoenix, AZ   85072-2040
Canadian address: P.O. Box 2800, Postal Station A,
5170 Yonge St., Willowdale, Ont.   M2N 6J3

Dark-Night Encounter

Betsy Page

Harlequin Books

TORONTO • NEW YORK • LONDON
AMSTERDAM • PARIS • SYDNEY • HAMBURG
STOCKHOLM • ATHENS • TOKYO • MILAN

Original hardcover edition published in 1983
by Mills & Boon Limited under the title *Dark-Night Stranger*

ISBN 0-373-02704-4

Harlequin Romance first edition July 1985

Copyright © 1983 by Betsy Page.
Philippine copyright 1983. Australian copyright 1983.

All rights reserved. Except for use in any review, the reproduction or utilization
of this work in whole or in part in any form by any electronic, mechanical
or other means, now known or hereafter invented, including xerography,
photocopying and recording, or in any information storage or retrieval system,
is forbidden without the permission of the publisher, Harlequin Enterprises
Limited, 225 Duncan Mill Road, Don Mills, Ontario, Canada M3B 3K9. All the
characters in this book have no existence outside the imagination of the
author and have no relation whatsoever to anyone bearing the same name
or names. They are not even distantly inspired by any individual known
or unknown to the author, and all the incidents are pure invention.

The Harlequin trademarks, consisting of the words HARLEQUIN ROMANCE
and the portrayal of a Harlequin, are trademarks of Harlequin Enterprises
Limited; the portrayal of a Harlequin is registered in the United States Patent
and Trademark Office and in the Canada Trade Marks Office.

Printed in U.S.A.

CHAPTER ONE

Jamie sat on the foot-high concrete lip of the drive-over bridge spanning the flowing river of water issuing from Bennett Spring less than a mile upstream. According to the brochure about the park which she had picked up in the camp store, the water poured out of the spring at an average rate of ninety-six million gallons a day. It then wound its way for a mile and a half through Bennett Spring State Park before emptying into the Niangua River. The Indians of centuries past had spoken of this spring, nestled in the Missouri Ozarks, as the Eye of the Earth and had believed that the water which poured continuously from its underground sources represented tears being shed for the future of the Osage people.

Her feet rested on one of the conduits through which the cold, fast-moving water poured out from beneath the bridge in a churning white foam. Strategically placed, the bait on the end of her fishing line lay at the edge of this violently swirling wetness. An overly large-brimmed straw hat shaded her head and shoulders from the hot June afternoon sun while round-lensed sunglasses protected her eyes. She wore a pair of shorts made by cutting the legs off of an old pair of faded denim jeans, a sleeveless blue print cotton blouse, and white tennis shoes without socks. Her long straight black hair was plaited into two thick pigtails which hung loosely down her back. To a passing stranger this slender yet well rounded young woman would probably be taken for eighteen rather than her actual age of twenty-four.

Jamie, however, was not interested in what anyone might be thinking about her as her mind once again left its preoccupation with the tranquil green beauty of her surroundings and returned to the problem which had plagued her for the past two weeks. Her father, James Bradley Kynter, had written successfully about fishing throughout the North American continent. In addition to several books, his monthly column, *Fishing with Old Duckbill*, had appeared in the issues of *Meadow and Brook*, a magazine edited by Jamie's uncle, Howard Kynter.

Duckbill—O. C. Duckbill to be complete—had been his byline. The 'O. C.' had been a word play with initials and the Duckbill had come from the nickname he had earned in college because of his protruding teeth. In the minds of his readership, the name conjured up the image of a veteran fisherman, and James Kynter had fitted the appellation from his faded jeans, patched green rubber waders, and lucky fishing hat to his red and black plaid shirts and thick full beard that sometimes got out of hand.

He had wanted a son, but when his wife died leaving him with a two-year-old daughter, he had taken the girl in hand and taught her all the things he had planned on teaching a son. Admittedly, during the greater part of the years while Jamie was growing up she had lived with her uncle and various housekeepers in a beautifully renovated old Colonial homestead the two brothers had purchased jointly following her mother's death. However, during her vacations and every summer she camped and fished with her father. Once in a while, beginning when she was in her early teens, he had encouraged her to write an occasional article and then submitted it under his byline. Her uncle knew of these little episodes of chicanery, but since the writing was similar and the articles interesting he had allowed them to go to press.

Then five years ago, when Jamie was only nineteen, James Kynter had died in a plane crash on his way to a secluded lake deep in the Canadian wilderness. She had been scheduled to accompany him but had caught a bad cold and he had made her stay at home, promising to take her with him the next time. His death had been a crushing blow and her uncle, in an effort to help her through this difficult time, had talked her into the deception which was now catching up with both of them.

Her father's insistence on anonymity had made it possible and, in her grief, Jamie had desperately wanted to keep some part of him alive. But it was a deception the predominantly male readership of *Meadow and Brook* might not take kindly to, and now the magazine had changed hands and the new owner was demanding to meet O. C. Duckbill. For the thousandth time, Jamie wished she could have been the son her father had wanted.

Breathing a sigh, she peered closely at the water below to check on her bait. Whatever the outcome, she would know soon. Yesterday when she made her weekly call to her uncle he had informed her that she had to be back home by Sunday at the latest. There was no way to put off the interview any longer. They would be meeting with Joshua Langley, the new owner, early Monday morning.

'Hi, Jamie!' a young male voice cut into her thoughts, directing her attention towards its owner, Joey Miller. Joey and his parents plus his little sister were camping next to her in the campgrounds near the spring. The boy was twelve years old and an ardent fisherman. He was up every morning, ready to cast his line in the moment the starting horn sounded at six-thirty sharp to mark the beginning of the fishing day. Then he fished almost continuously for the next fourteen hours until the quitting signal was sounded. During the three days she had been in the park, he had caught four trout each day, just one less than the allotted limit of five.

'Hi,' she returned his greeting with a smile.

'Mind if I join you?'

'Not at all.' She was glad to have company to keep her mind off of Monday morning's meeting. 'How have you done so far today?'

'Got four, so far,' he answered with a delighted grin. 'What are you fishing with?'

'I'm trying a cheese bait I bought at the camp store. Want to use some?' she offered. Although Jamie had her own recipe for a dough bait, it was her practice to try the available commercial products for informational purposes to be incorporated into her column. Fishing for trout with bait at all was unusual for her. However, this park, as well as others she had encountered this summer in her efforts to experience family camping areas with fishing as the main source of amusement, provided for a variety of fishing tastes. The spring branch flowing through the park had been divided into three zones, each with specifically designated types of lures or baits, and she felt that to be thorough she should fish in each zone.

'No, thanks. I have some cheese bread I want to try,' the boy replied, seating himself several feet away.

The bridge was nearly deserted at this time of the day when the sun made it uncomfortable for those who did not relish the afternoon heat. The early morning was very different. Not only did fishermen, women and children stand shoulder to shoulder along this concrete structure waiting impatiently for the starting signal to be sounded, but a band of heartier souls waded out into the water to form a line just beyond the wild swirling wetness issuing from beneath the bridge. This particular spot was not unique either. All the prime fishing holes up and down the spring branch were similarly populated. The major reason people were willing to brave the chill dawn air and the crowded conditions was that the stream was restocked each night with fish from the hatchery on the park grounds, and it was these novice trout which provided the lure for the populace.

Jamie had chosen to observe rather than participate in this frantic early morning activity. She found it fascinating to watch as the signal sounded and dozens of lines hit the water simultaneously, some crossing others to end in tangled messes, some falling short of their mark, while still others brought home the trophy. But because she did not like crowds, what was the most curious part to her was how much fun the participants had even with the problems a group that size presented.

Suddenly, an unexpectedly strong breeze swept across the water, forcing her to make a grab for her hat. As she did so, her eyes fell on a dark-haired man leaning against the base of a tree on the high bank to her right. He was of slightly more than average height and, from the way the white knit shirt he wore fitted across his chest, it was obvious he was in excellent physical condition. He was watching her, a look of masculine appreciation on his face. Normally a man's attentions would not have bothered her, but in this case she intuitively sensed danger. Even in his leisurely stance he had an air of authority and experience. Reacting to a strong instinct for self-preservation, she frowned at him dissuasively. Nodding his head in her direction as if to say 'as you wish', he sauntered off upstream. Much to her shock, Jamie suddenly felt deserted. While telling herself that it was simply her concern over the upcoming meeting with Mr Langley that had caused her to react so intensely to a total stranger, she found herself fighting an almost uncontrollable urge to glance over her shoulder in the direction in which the man had walked.

Just as her head was about to turn of its own volition her line tightened, demanding her concentration as a nice-sized trout bent her pole in its fight for freedom. As a general rule, Jamie fished with an unbarbed hook. This allowed her the option of freeing her catch unharmed if she should choose to do so, because as much as she enjoyed eating the fruits of her labour, there was a limit as to how many fish any one person could consume. Landing her prize, she decided to keep this one and stop for the day.

Walking back to her car, she noticed that the sky looked threatening and decided to give herself a treat rather than get caught cooking in the rain. Changing direction, she headed towards the sprawling wooden dining lodge. On their menu they offered to prepare your own freshly caught trout and serve it to you with vegetables and salad for a moderate sum, and she reasoned that she owed it to her readers to try out this aspect of their service. Arranging to return at seven, she left her catch and drove back to her campsite.

The trip back to Pennsylvania would take two days and it was already Thursday. If she wanted a full day of rest before the fateful Monday meeting, she would have to leave sometime the following morning. Black clouds rolled above her, darkening the sky in an ominous manner. Because packing in the rain was not one of her favourite pastimes, she spent the remainder of the afternoon loading her equipment into the back of her compact Buick stationwagon. She left only her tent, sleeping bag and a flashlight to be thrown in the following morning.

That evening, while dining on the deliciously prepared meal she found herself observing the other diners with more than an abstract interest. With this discovery came the realisation that she was actually trying to spot the dark-haired man she had seen from the bridge earlier in the day. You aren't thinking of speaking to him! she scolded herself in an effort to shake the peculiar anticipatory feeling which prevailed within her.

The fact that she had even considered speaking to him disturbed her. Travelling alone, she had, out of a sense of self-protection, always made it a rule to avoid possible relationships with lone men. It would be too easy to find herself caught in a compromising circumstance from which escape might prove difficult if not impossible. Again she blamed her anxiety over the coming meeting with Joshua Langley for her overreaction to the stranger under the tree. However, she could not totally disregard the sense of disappointment which came over her when the time to leave arrived and he had not made an appearance. Telling herself that he probably had a wife and four children, she pulled on her raincoat in preparation for facing the downpour outside. The thought which was supposed to help her mood did not.

The rain was still coming down steadily and heavily when she parked within a couple of feet of the entrance to her tent. Discarding her wet raincoat in the car, she dashed into the canvas shelter. Luckily it was sturdy and she had waterproofed it well. Lying in the dark, listening to the pelting raindrops, she tried to find peace in sleep. What difference did it make how her new employer took the news that she was a woman, or even how the male readership took it? It wasn't the Dark Ages any more. With all the new women's magazines on the market today she could find a job working for one of them. She was a very good writer. Finally she dozed off, the last image in her mind being that of a dark stranger who nodded and walked away never to be seen again.

'Come on, sleepyhead, wake up!' the male voice penetrating her sleep clogged mind commanded. A large hand shook her roughly and she felt the wetness from outside blowing in on her.

Rolling over, she opened her eyes, only to be blinded by the beam of a flashlight being shone directly on to her face. 'Turn that thing off!' she demanded hotly.

'It is you.' The words were a murmur, barely audible above the sounds of the storm as the speaker confirmed a hitherto questionable fact to himself. Then in a firmer tone, the interloper said, 'All right, the light isn't on you. Now, where's the boy—your brother, I assume, since you're too young for him to be your son?'

'What boy?' Jamie questioned in a state of confusion, her mind still groggy as she opened her eyes slowly to determine that the light had been averted. Picking up her own flashlight, she turned it on her intruder, only to find herself seriously wondering if she wasn't actually dreaming all of this. The man standing in the entrance of her tent, rain rolling in streams down his mackintosh, was the man from the river bank who had occupied so much of her mind these past few hours. However, the cold dampness blowing in on her was too real to be a figment of her imagination.

The man had apparently taken a closer look around the inside of her tent because instead of answering her question he said in a disapproving tone, 'You're here all alone.'

'Yes, I'm here all alone,' she snapped back defensively. 'And I want to know what boy you're talking about.'

'The boy on the bridge,' the stranger responded absently as if the question was now obsolete and needed no reply, his attention focused fully on the indignant dark-haired girl encased in her sleeping bag leaning on an elbow glaring up at him.

Jamie felt suddenly vulnerable. 'He's my neighbour in the next tent,' she threw at him, fighting the unsettling effect the man was having on her. 'And why in the world are you looking for him in the middle of the night in a rainstorm?'

'I wasn't actually looking for him.' An amused note entered the man's voice. 'You look like a tigress with those green eyes flashing like that.'

'Mister, get out of my tent!' Jamie clutched her flashlight more securely in the event she might need it for a weapon.

'Dangerous, too,' he mused, a slow grin on his face as he had noticed her hand tighten on the instrument. Then as if recalling a more important matter, his face became serious. 'There's been close to three inches of rain in the park and more above us. The Park Rangers are afraid of a flash-flood and are asking the campers in this campground to evacuate to higher ground.'

'You're not a Park Ranger.'

'No, I'm not. I was talking to one when the word came in and rode over with him to see if I could help.'

'All right,' she said, her hand seeking the tab of the zipper on her sleeping bag. 'You've delivered your message, now you can leave.' In her angry confusion, she had begun unzipping the protective covering, forgetting that beneath she was clad only in a tee-shirt and panties. As the cold wind hit her exposed thigh she came to an abrupt halt.

'Zipper stuck?' the man asked, the amusement back in his voice. 'Maybe I could be of some help.' He started towards her.

'You can help by getting out of here and letting me get dressed.' Her voice was cool as ice masking a nervous trembling inside caused by the thought of the man's hands so near her skin.

'Yes, ma'am,' he chuckled, and was gone as suddenly as he had arrived.

Quickly Jamie climbed out of the warmth of her sleeping bag and into her jeans, chiding herself for leaving her rain slicker in the car, although in this kind of downpour even it would not have kept her totally dry. Deciding that it was senseless to take the time to change into her blouse and bra since everything she was wearing was sure to get soaked in the process of taking down the tent, she rolled the unnecessary articles up into the sleeping bag. She would wear the tee-shirt, in which she had been sleeping, with her jeans. Once the tent was successfully stowed she would change into the dry set of clothes she kept for emergencies in the blue satchel on the back seat of her car.

Leaving the safety of her canvas shelter, she ran to the station wagon and threw her sleeping bag in on all the other equipment. When she returned to the tent and began pulling up stakes, the stranger again materialised. He fell into step beside her, surprising her by how well they worked together. As they finished throwing the wet canvas, poles and stakes in on the floor of the back seat of her car, away from the dry equipment, she turned to thank him, only to discover he was on his way to help the Millers. They were struggling with their much larger cabin size tent plus a netted eating canopy. Already soaked to the skin, she saw no hurry to get out of the cold rain since she couldn't get any wetter, so she too joined the Millers to give them a hand. It was a messy job, and by the time the couple and their children plus their equipment were in their car and on their way, the campground was practically deserted.

'Mind giving me a ride back to my camper?' the dark-eyed stranger requested as she started back towards her car.

'No, of course not.' She felt she owed him that much for all the help he had been to both herself and the Millers. It wasn't until she tried to fit the key into the ignition that she realised she was shivering uncontrollably. Soaked to the skin as she was, the cold winds accompanying the chilly rain had penetrated her entire body.

The man took the keys from her icy fingers and walking around to the driver's side made her move over as he climbed in and took charge of the wheel. 'You should have a raincoat. You'll lucky if you don't catch pneumonia.'

'I do have a raincoat. It's just that it was in the car and I didn't expect to be out in that downpour for so long.' Her teeth were chattering so badly she had trouble delivering this defensive statement.

He said nothing. His jaw set in a hard line, he manoeuvred the car out of the campground and along the road past the rapidly rising river. Ten minutes later they came to a halt beside a large Winnebago. 'Do you have any dry clothes convenient?' he asked.

By this time Jamie was shaking violently. 'In the blue satchel.' She indicated the piece of luggage on the back seat with a twist of her head.

The man grabbed the small piece of luggage and leaving the car, opened the door of the motor home and tossed it inside. Returning to the car, he opened the passenger door and gathering Jamie up into his arms, started to carry her towards his camper.

'Put me down!' she demanded.

'Shut up,' came his retort. 'Little girls who don't know how to take care of themselves shouldn't be allowed out on their own.'

Jamie's cheeks flushed red as she clamped her lips together and tried to control her shivering.

'The electricity is off because of the storm,' he told her coldly, obviously annoyed by the nuisance both she and the storm had become, as he set her down in a standing position between the couch and the bench-flanked table.

Jamie stood selfconsciously, her wet clothes clinging to her like a second skin while the carpet under and around her began to feel soggy. The man removed his mackintosh, hanging it on the door to drip on the rubber-covered steps above his muddy boots. 'You travel alone much?' he asked as the light from his flashlight fell on her upper torso where the rain-soaked tee-shirt left very little to the imagination.

She could not see his face but the question sparked a flame of fear. 'No, not much. Usually my husband accompanies me,' she lied. For a long moment the light was strong on her face as if he was trying to read the truth in her features, then it travelled quickly down to her feet where the carpet was darkening in an ever-increasing circle around her.

'Take off those wet tennis shoes.' It was a command, and she obeyed.

Picking them up, he tossed the dirty canvas footwear down beside his boots. 'You'll need to warm up some before you can manage to change,' he said, the flashlight again playing over her shivering body, 'unless you're willing to let me help you.'

There had been only the slightest suggestiveness in his tone, but Jamie tensed, prepared to do battle if necessary, although from the way he had so easily carried her, she knew she would stand no chance against his brute strength. 'No,' she rejected the proposal firmly, wrapping her arms around herself in an effort to regain some control over her shaking body.

The man moved to the other side of the doorway and using the flashlight to find the latch on an upper cupboard pulled out a blanket and tossed it over on to the couch. 'Then wrap up in that.'

'I'll just get it wet too,' she protested, close to tears from the cold and fear.

'Strip first.' It was another command, but this time she hesitated. Swallowing the lump rising in her throat, she wondered if she could make her chilled cramped legs carry her past the man and out of this gilded trap. 'Strip!' This time there was a threat in his voice and she knew that if she did not obey, he intended to assist her.

A flash of lightning momentarily illuminated the interior of the camper. 'You turn around,' she stipulated.

With an impatient shrug he did as she requested. Jamie peeled the soggy clothes from her body as rapidly as her numb fingers would allow, then wrapped herself securely in the heavy blanket. Seating herself on the sofa, curling her feet up under her in an effort to thaw out her toes, she forced her voice to sound calmly aloof as she said, 'You can turn round now.'

Almost as if it were a physical contact, she felt his eyes rest on her for a moment. Then, picking up her discarded clothing, he carried the dripping articles into the compact bathroom and dropped them into the shower stall. As he found his way around the camper by the use of his flashlight, Jamie followed his movements much like a prey might observe its stalker searching for a means of escape. From a closet across from what she judged to be the refrigerator, he extracted a pair of jeans and a shirt. 'I'm a little wet myself,' he said, obviously conscious of her attention. 'I intend to change. You may watch if you wish.'

Quickly, she averted her head as a blush gave colour to her pale face. The man was an arrogant bore! The back of the blanket was beginning to feel damp and she realised that her thick wet pigtails were to blame. Freeing her arms, she wound the heavy material more securely around her bosom, then attempting to hold it in place with her chin, she caught one of the pigtails and unfastening the elastic holding it together, began to disentangle the braided hair. The blanket slipped, forcing her to abandon her task to make a grab for the unco-operative covering.

'I'll do that.' The cushion next to her sank under the man's weight. His hand brushed her bare shoulder as it moved to capture the hank of hair on which she had been working, causing a chill unrelated to the cold to sweep over her.

'I can manage,' she protested.

'Don't worry. Pigtails are my speciality,' he said as he finished with the first and started on the second. 'I have two long-haired kid sisters. Of course they're not kids any longer.'

Jamie started to point out that she was not his sister nor a kid, then swallowed her retort. She felt certain he was already well aware she was no child, and if he wanted to consider her a sister that was fine with her.

Once the hair was free he produced a towel and began rubbing it vigorously. After a while, however, his technique became gentler and the back of his hand came into more and more contact with her shoulders and neck.

A warmth she had never experienced before heated her body. She found it difficult to think. Frightened by this new sensation, she looked around, searching for some means of escaping the man's disturbing touch. 'I thought vehicles this expensive came with an auxiliary generator,' she blurted out, her voice sounding stilted rather than casual as she had planned.

'You're right.' He paused, his hands resting on the sensitive curve at the back of her neck. 'I didn't think about that. This is the first trip I've taken in this apartment on wheels, as the salesman called it.' Still he made no move to leave her side.

Jamie tensed.

'You're as tight as a violin string.' Encasing her hair loosely in the towel, he began to massage her neck and bare shoulders. His hands moved expertly, sensually as they worked their way further and further down her spine.

She fought for control, but the man made it difficult. His warm breath played on her skin and the urge to lean back against him and allow his arms to encircle her was great. However, her sense of self-preservation was greater. She knew she had to get away, but clad only in a blanket, she felt stymied. 'I'm not used to sitting around in the dark with a total stranger,' she said, her tone implying that she would be much more co-operative if he would rectify this condition.

'If light will help you relax, then your wish is my command.'

As he moved to the front of the vehicle, she rose and grabbing her satchel made a dash for the bathroom, finding her way in the dark through sheer instinct. The light came on as she pulled the door closed and snapped the lock. Her fingers were now completely defrosted. She changed quickly, but her hand froze on the door when the time came to re-enter the main body of the camper. However there was no other way out and she didn't intend to spend the rest of her life in the cramped bathroom. Squaring her shoulders, she opened the door and stepped out.

'Just toss the blanket on the bed.' With a nod, the man indicated the double bed directly beside her. There was a half amused, half angry gleam in his eyes as he stood in the narrow passage by the stove blocking her path. 'I thought you might like some coffee.'

'I really have to be on my way.' Her voice shook only slightly as she dropped the blanket as requested. 'Thank you for your help.' Spotting her car keys on the near counter, she slipped them into her pocket and moved towards the door. The knuckles of the hand which gripped the satchel were white with strain.

'The light doesn't seem to have relaxed you at all.'

Jamie wetted her lips but said nothing.

He moved towards her like an animal closing in on its prey. Before she could act, she was caught. His body held her against the door of the bathroom while his hands captured her face turning it upward towards his descending mouth. She steeled herself for the onslaught, dropping the satchel to press her hands against his hard frame while tears of fear escaped from the corners of her eyes. How could she have been so naïve as to get herself into this situation!

There was no onslaught. She felt only the slightest brush of his lips before he released her. Stepping, back, he asked contemptuously. 'Did you ever consider fainting?'

Her eyes popped open in shock.

'Little girls,' he continued drily, 'shouldn't play adult games. They could find themselves in a great deal of trouble.'

Anger flared. How dared he set himself up as her mentor! 'I'm not a little girl!'

'Oh, no?' A half smile twisted one corner of his mouth. Suddenly she found herself once again in his arms, only this time his mouth found hers. After a moment's useless struggle she stood rigid, determined to endure his embrace with aloof indifference.

The kiss, which began savagely as if he was teaching her not to contradict him, gradually softened, becoming coaxing, more demanding of her participation. Her resolve weakened under this gentler persuasion. His hands caressed her, moving expertly over the soft contours of her body, melting her stiffness and causing her to yield, blending her length into his as if they were one.

His lips left her mouth to travel down the sensitive cords of her neck, sparking fires of longing never before ignited. Circling her arms around him, Jamie clung to him for support as an awakening hunger filled her.

'Maybe I did misjudge you.' His voice was low and husky and his breathing ragged. 'It must have been the pigtails.' Again his mouth sought hers for a newer, deeper assault which she greeted with all the yearning need of newly born desire.

A moan of regret escaped from her when he once again abandoned her lips to feather kisses over her face.

'When does that husband of yours expect you home?' he asked lazily, his mouth moving against the hollow of her neck as he spoke. 'Can you stay a day or two?'

'No, I have to start home soon.' Her words were filled with regret.

'But not right this minute.' He mocked her need to leave.

Home! The word conjured up images of her uncle, causing a semblance of sanity to return. What was she doing in a stranger's arms in the middle of the night? The question exploded in her brain, demanding an answer she could not provide.

The man's hold was loose. With one quick twist she was free. 'I have to leave now. Right now,' she stammered, backing towards the door. The latch gave. Practically falling over his boots, she leaped from the camper and dashed for her car. Fishing her keys out of her pocket, she somehow managed to fit the correct one into the ignition. Her hands were shaking violently as she turned it and pressed on the gas. The motor refused to start.

'It's probably flooded,' the man noted cynically as he opened the door on the passenger side.

Jamie's tear-filled eyes met his dark gaze with a look of animal fear.

'You forgot these.' He tossed her shoes and satchel on to the front seat, then slamming the door closed, walked away.

The dam burst. Mingled tears of anger, frustration, humiliation, and regret poured down her cheeks. She tried the engine again, and this time it started. Wiping at her face with balled fists, she guided the car away from the camper, away from the stranger who had aroused emotions of frightening proportions within her.

Pulling into the parking lot across from the camp store to hunt for a pair of dry shoes, she noticed for the first time that the rain had ceased. Her search successful, she decided to drive through to St Louis. She would find a motel room there and get some rest. As she drove through the pitch black night, she tried to convince herself that she was braving the wet, hazardous roads because she was anxious to return home. But a part of her knew it was because she had a strong need to put distance between herself and the dark-eyed man.

She slept a few hours in St Louis, then drove across Illinois and Indiana before stopping for the night near Dayton, Ohio. The flat, fertile farmlands alternating with rolling wooded stretches of more rugged terrain helped to sooth her shattered nerves. However, every once in a while, the image of the dark-haired, dark-eyed stranger would sneak into her mind. Vividly, as if she could actually feel his touch, she would remember how his lips had tasted and how his arms had felt as they held her.

She stayed in motels on the way home, hoping that their stark modernism would help erase the drama of her midnight encounter in the wilderness. But still the stranger commanded her dreams. Sometimes he was a villain, while at others he merely mocked her. Alternately she hated him and yearned for him. On Saturday morning she awoke as exhausted as when she had first lain down.

Telling herself that at home in her own bed she would rest better and be able to put Thursday night behind her, she pushed herself to complete this last eleven-hour leg of her journey. It was ridiculous of her to allow the episode to haunt her. She tried to look on it as a learning experience. She had played with fire and, luckily, had managed to escape unscathed. Unscathed? Was she truly, or would those piercing eyes always remain in her memory, taunting her?

The flat corn, wheat, and bean fields of Ohio gradually gave way to the foothills of the Appalachians as she neared Wheeling, West Virginia. By the time she was in Pennsylvania, she was driving through the heart of the mountain range. The Appalachians were an ancient range worn down by time and the massive glaciers of the Ice Age. There were no year-round snow-covered peaks reaching up beyond the clouds as one would see in the Rockies out west. Even so, Jamie loved these gentle mountains with their towns of all sizes and complexions nestled in the valleys along the Turnpike.

Taking the Valley Forge exit, she drove another half hour through a sparsely populated region before finally turning into the long drive of the fifty-acre tract belonging to her and her uncle. Never had the sight of the native stone, eighteenth-century farmhouse looked so inviting.

Her uncle was not home and she guessed that he was dining with friends or possibly with one of the many women who found the fifty-two-year-old, peppered grey-haired, athletic bachelor more than a little charming. She had often wondered why Howard Kynter had never married and finally had asked him. 'I'm a man who's married to his work,' he had told her. 'No woman can be happy playing second fiddle to a magazine.'

As much as she loved him, she was glad of the reprieve. Making light conversation about her trip when she felt so drained would have been nearly impossible. Lugging the wet tent out of the car, she set it up to dry on the long sloping back lawn. Her sleeping bag she threw over two lawn chairs pushed together. Then going inside, she showered and climbed into her safe comfortable bed, leaving the rest of the equipment until the next day to be unpacked.

But even here in her private haven the stranger penetrated her subconscious, weaving in and out of her dreams.

CHAPTER TWO

Monday morning arrived bright and sunshiny. However, as Jamie sat across the breakfast table from her uncle, a half-eaten slice of toast on her plate, her mind was not occupied with the sunshine outside. Instead she was recalling a cold rainy night. When she had told her uncle about the storm, she had omitted mentioning the stranger who continued to find his way into her thoughts. It was a bittersweet memory. He had awakened a depth of emotion within her she had not known existed, yet he had also embarrassed and humiliated her. She could never have faced him again without feeling foolish and resentful. Still, somewhere deep inside, the thought of never seeing him again caused a twinge of pain.

'You've seemed distracted since you returned home from this last trip,' Howard Kynter remarked, observing his niece with a concerned expression on his face. 'I hope you aren't worried about this interview with Joshua Langley.'

'What?' Jamie forced her mind back to the present. Then catching the latter part of the question, she said, 'Maybe, a little.'

'You shouldn't be. The man is young and has lots of modern ideas.'

'Let's just hope one of them is women fishing experts.' Pushing her chair back from the table, she rose. 'I think I'll go upstairs and check my make-up once more.'

'You look fine. In fact, you look stunning.'

'And you're prejudiced. Perhaps I should wear my waders and carry a fishing pole and tackle box I might look more authentic,' she suggested playfully.

'That dress will do just fine.' Watching her go out, Howard breathed a silent sigh of relief, grateful that she had retained her sense of humour. He wouldn't admit it to her, but he was concerned about her future with *Meadow and Brook*. He knew he could not protect her for ever. But he felt responsible. He had got her into this deception in the first place.

Standing in front of the full-length mirror attached to her bedroom door, Jamie made a final survey of herself. Lipstick was the only make-up she had applied, her delicately summer-tanned complexion needing nothing more. Her features were well shaped, her nose small and her lips full, but it was her green eyes matched with her coal black hair that caught people's attention. Today she had pulled the long, straight tresses into a ponytail which she had then plaited, producing a thick pigtail hanging down to the middle of her back. A Kelly green ribbon had been worked into the heavy braid with a bow of the same colour neatly tied on the end. The green of the ribbon matched the green in her white and green striped shirtwaist-style dress. She had chosen white heeled sandals and a white shoulder-string bag to complete her attire.

'I'm as ready as I'll ever be,' she muttered. Rewarding herself with a grimace, she hurried back to her uncle, who was waiting impatiently by the front door.

'Grace called a minute ago,' he said as he hurried her out to the car.

She knew he meant Grace Adams, his secretary for the past twenty years. 'I heard the phone ring. What did she want?'

'It would appear that Mr Joshua Langley is as anxious to have this interview as you are to avoid it. He's already arrived and she has Ray showing him around.'

Giving her uncle an amused raised eyebrow look, Jamie said in a jokingly philosophical tone, 'Breaking in new publishers is never easy.'

Howard chuckled. 'You've been a real joy to me in my old age.'

'I was under the impression that you were still middle-aged. When did you become old?' she chided affectionately.

'Whenever I see you all dressed up, I realise you're not a little girl any longer and suddenly I feel ancient.'

'Ancient? I can't believe you've gone from old to ancient in only two minutes!'

'Don't worry. I'll be back to oldish middle-age by the time we reach the office.'

'Good. Because we don't have time to stop and buy you a cane to totter in on,' she laughed, and he joined her.

Minutes later they were walking rapidly down the carpeted corridor which led to his office. 'I'll page Ray and have him bring Mr Langley right up,' said Grace as they approached her desk. Howard nodded and passed through to his office while Grace held Jamie back. Of all the people who worked for the magazine, she was the only one Howard had trusted with his niece's secret. 'I've held off pulling one of your standby articles out of the file because you said you wanted to use the current material you were gathering on your travels this summer, but I need your column right away.'

'I know.' There was a hint of distress in Jamie's voice. She had tried to write several times during her stops on the way home and on the previous evening had sat in front of her typewriter for three hours, but had come up with nothing usable. The image of the stranger had continued to interrupt her thoughts. 'I'll bring it in tomorrow.'

'Is anything wrong? You know that if you ever need a woman to talk to, you can come to me.'

'I'm just a little nervous about this morning, but thank you for your concern.' Jamie had held her own counsel for too many years to change now.

'You don't have anything to be nervous about,' Grace assured her, then picking up the phone, paged Ray Harley.

Jamie joined her uncle in his office. Too tense to sit,

she wandered over to the window and gazed out on the carefully manicured lawn.

'Mr Kynter,' an authoritative male voice said as the door opened, and the man they were expecting entered. 'I'm Joshua Langley, and I'm pleased to be meeting you face to face at last.'

Jamie's back stiffened as her heart seemed to stop beating momentarily. It couldn't be. It just couldn't be! Telling herself that lots of people sound the same, she turned slowly.

Howard Kynter moved around his desk to shake hands with the new owner of the magazine. 'It's a pleasure to meet you, too. And I would like to introduce my niece, Jamie Beth Kynter.'

'Mrs Kynter.' The man pronounced her name in a polite indifferent manner. He wore a three-piece suit in place of the jeans and knit shirt, but she would have recognised those mocking eyes anywhere.

'It's Miss Kynter,' Howard corrected.

'Miss Jamie Beth Kynter.' This time, as he said her name, Joshua Langley approached Jamie.

Moving of its own volition, her hand met his in a civil handshake which lasted only a moment but brought back a flood of memories and emotions that threatened to overwhelm her. She swallowed, willing herself to speak, but no words would come out.

'Are you going to faint, now?' The question laced with ridicule was asked quietly, for her ears only.

'Not over you. Not ever,' she muttered back through a forced smile.

'Why don't we all sit down?' Howard suggested, joining them by the window. 'I've asked Grace to send in some coffee.' He led the way to a couch and chair grouping.

Jamie moved as if she were a robot following instructions. This couldn't be happening. She prayed she would wake up any minute and discover it was all nothing more than a nightmare. Her uncle seated himself in one of the leather-upholstered chairs and she quickly claimed the other, leaving Joshua Langley the couch. It was a mistake. She realised that as soon as he positioned himself directly across from her. He was obviously enjoying her discomfort. A deep fury directed towards the man flamed inside her.

'Jamie has been a little nervous about meeting you, Mr Langley,' said Howard, confused by his niece's reticence and feeling the need to offer some sort of explanation.

'Please, call me Josh, Howard,' Joshua Langley requested, removing his gaze from Jamie momentarily to address her uncle, then returning it to the female in front of him. 'And why should Miss Kynter be nervous about meeting me? In fact, why am I meeting Miss Kynter at all? I thought I was to meet O. C. Duckbill to discuss some publicity ideas I have.'

'Before I answer your questions, I'd like to know if you took the trip we discussed.' In an aside to Jamie, Howard explained, 'Josh expressed a desire to see Duckbill in action, and although I couldn't in good conscience provide him with a description of our reclusive columnist, I did agree to give him Duckbill's itinerary.'

'I was only able to make the Bennett Spring stop.' Josh's manner was curt. 'And although I spent some time watching several men I felt were skilled enough and close to the right age to be O. C. Duckbill, I notice that none of them are here this morning.'

'Perhaps if you'll try to picture my niece in a pair of blue jeans and a shirt and probably pigtails, you might recall seeing her there,' Howard suggested.

The mention of pigtails caused Jamie to fidget as Josh's eyes travelled over her in a disquieting inspection. 'Maybe if Miss Kynter—Jamie—will stand and turn . . .'

'I'll do no such thing!' she retorted indignantly.

A slow smile which did not reach his eyes spread over

Josh Langley's features. 'As a matter of fact, I do believe I saw a woman, a girl, who resembled your niece.'

'And perhaps you noticed how skilful she was,' Howard persisted.

'Skilful?' Josh's dark eyes scrutinised Jamie even more closely. 'Yes, I suppose you could say she was skilful.'

Swallowing hard, Jamie heard a great deal more in those words than her uncle could ever suspect. She felt like finding a hole and crawling into it but there were none available. In her own self-defence, the thought occurred to her that Josh Langley should crawl back under his rock instead. Maybe she hadn't behaved as properly as a lady should behave, but then he hadn't been exactly a gentleman either, and he certainly wasn't exhibiting any signs of chivalry by throwing innuendoes and reminders of her improprieties in her face.

Suddenly, as if he had grown tired of playing games, Josh shifted his full attention towards her uncle. 'I don't know what you're leading up to, Howard, but I wish you'd spit it out. I went to Bennett Spring to observe O. C. Duckbill and I saw your niece. Since Miss Kynter is obviously not old enough to have written a twenty-year-old column, I don't see the connection.'

'Jamie's father originated the O. C. Duckbill column,' Howard began. 'He . . .'

'Miss Kynter,' Josh interrupted with a frown.

'My father died several years ago,' Jamie cut Josh off. She sensed he was about to mention that she had been at Bennett Spring alone, and although her uncle might not have caught on right away, after he had thought about it he would wonder how a man who purportedly could barely recall a woman he observed a few days earlier knew so much about her. 'And I've been writing the column ever since.'

'You're O. C. Duckbill?' There was something almost accusatory in the way he looked at her.

'For the past five years,' she confirmed, her back straight and her chin held high.

'You're not exactly what I or, I might add, our readers had in mind,' Josh pointed out, his frown deepening.

'Jamie is an excellent writer and an expert in her field.' Howard came to his niece's defence. 'I wouldn't have talked her into continuing the column if I hadn't believed in her abilities. My brother trained her in both fishing and writing. He also provided her with plenty of opportunities to practise both as she grew up.'

'And her mother allows her to travel around the country alone?' There was condemnation in Josh's voice.

'I'm over twenty-one,' she told him frigidly.

'Her mother died when Jamie was two,' Howard explained in a calmer tone. 'It's I who allow her to travel alone. She's camped since she was very young and I trust her to know how to take care of herself.'

Josh's eyes darkened cynically. It was the last straw for Jamie. The man could criticise her. Perhaps she deserved his contempt, but her uncle did not. Besides, who did he think he was anyway, to sit in judgment on them? In a voice like ice water, she said, 'Mr Langley, I'm a good writer. I realise that our little deception was not completely ethical—however, it was done with the best of intentions. My father's death was devastating for me, and my uncle saw this as a way of getting me through the crisis. I saw it as a way of keeping some part of my father alive—a continuing memorial, so to speak. If you want to fire me or run me out of town on a rail, say so, but don't criticise my uncle.'

'Perhaps it would be better to continue this discussion at another time,' Howard suggested, his gaze shifting from his niece to Josh and back again as the tension in the room became so thick it could be cut with a knife.

Ignoring him, Josh kept his attention riveted on the black-haired female who glared at him with jade green eyes. 'I apologise, Miss Kynter. You're perfectly right.

How you and your uncle choose to live your lives is none of my business.'

'That's right, Mr Langley, it's none of your concern,' she confirmed tightly. 'None at all.'

Thunder rolled across his face as he met her defiant gaze in silence. Then as if a door had closed, his expression became shuttered. 'I suppose,' he addressed Howard, his manner once again strictly businesslike, 'you would prefer that I allow this deception to continue.'

'That's up to you,' Howard replied, wondering what had gone wrong. He had spoken to Josh Langley many times over the phone and had always found him relatively easy to get along with. Then there was Jamie. He had never seen his niece act this way. 'Jamie is a talented writer. If you feel the deception must be made public and that our readers will react adversely, then I'm certain she can find another job with a magazine that has a more general readership.'

'I'm certain she could.' Josh's tone was pensive. 'I apologise if I was rude, but this has been a shock. The magazine, as I'm sure you're aware, needs a publicity boost to compete in today's market. I had hoped to enlist O. C. Duckbill in this capacity. Let me think about this for a couple of days.' Extending his hand, he rose to leave.

Howard accepted the handshake, relieved that the interview had not ended in a total catastrophe. In fact, Josh had been very reasonable. Now if Jamie would behave . . .

'Miss Kynter.' Josh extended his hand in her direction.

Not wanting to appear petty, she accepted the handshake. Even in her anger, his touch elicited a disturbingly sensual response deep within her. Withdrawing her hand, she wondered if it wouldn't be better for her to leave *Meadow and Brook* and put as much distance between herself and Mr Joshua Langley as possible.

'Jamie, what in the world has gotten into you?'

Howard asked, the moment Josh was out the door. There was a worried edge to his tone.

'I'm sorry,' she apologised, not knowing how to explain without going into the whole story, and that she refused to do.

'You're over wrought. I've been neglecting you.'

'No, you haven't. It's just me. I'm probably going through another one of those growing states.'

'I thought those ended with adolescence.'

'If you'd read any of the new psychology magazines, you would know they're finding new ones every day.'

'Maybe. Maybe,' he murmured, watching her closely.

'I'd like to go home now,' she said. 'I have a splitting headache.'

'Why don't you make an appointment to see Dr Evans? You could be coming down with something,' he suggested.

'If I'm coming down with anything, he won't be able to stop it. All he'll do is tell me to take a couple of aspirin and go to bed, and that's what I intend to do anyway. Please, just drive me home.'

They were on their way out of the building when Ray Harley caught up with them. 'Howard, there's a problem that needs your immediate attention,' the man insisted.

'I have to take my niece home, she isn't feeling well. Can't it wait?' Howard frowned.

'I don't think so.' Ray shook his head in a negative gesture.

'If Miss Kynter doesn't object, I would be happy to take her home,' Josh's voice sounded from behind Jamie.

'I thought you'd left.' The words were out before she realised she had spoken.

'I stopped by Ray's office to thank him for the tour this morning,' he explained, ignoring her bluntness. 'Now, what about my offer? May I escort you home?'

'Jamie's not feeling well,' Howard interjected, not at

all sure it would be prudent to allow her time alone with Josh considering her present frame for mind. 'I wouldn't want to be accused of exposing my new employer to anything contagious.'

'I'm willing to take the risk. You're needed here. I promise to take very good care of her.'

Tilting her head back, Jamie looked up into the hard chiselled features of the face that had haunted her both awake and asleep. She could not run for ever; sooner or later she would have to face him alone. 'Uncle, you take care of your problems,' she told him.

'Are you sure?' Howard's expression was one of anxiety mingled with relief. He didn't want Jamie upset any more than she already was, but he also hated to leave when there was even a hint of trouble at the magazine.

'Positive.' Giving him a farewell hug, she accepted Josh's arm and allowed him to escort her out of the building. Even with the thickness of his jacket between her hand and his skin, she could feel his body warmth penetrate into her, recalling memories of fear, humiliation and longing. Once outside, she immediately broke the contact.

'The magazine means a great deal to your uncle,' he observed as he held the car door open for her.

'It is important to him,' she confirmed as he climbed into the driver's seat.

'More important than his niece?'

'No!' Her eyes glittered with rage. 'No, that's not true. He, like my father, simply treats me more like a man would treat a son than a daughter. He doesn't subject me to the over-protective double standards many people force on women.' Her hand fell on the door handle.

'You're free to leave.' The threat in his voice was inconsistent with his words. 'There are, however, answers to certain questions I must have before I can make my decision concerning your column. I believe you might prefer to give them to me privately rather than in front of your uncle.'

'Mr Langley, I'm too much of a lady to tell you what you can do with your job, but I'm sure you get the picture.' Opening the door, she started to step out.

'Don't be too hasty,' he cautioned. 'I've come to think of you and your uncle as a team—at least, for the moment.'

She froze. The implication was explicit. 'You wouldn't!'

'Fire your uncle? Maybe not. Then again, he was not only involved but was, by his own admission, the instigator of your little deception. If on learning the truth, the mostly male readership of our magazine feel they've been hoodwinked into taking advice from a mere girl and resent it, I might be forced to take drastic action.'

'I can't believe they'd be so chauvinistic.' In spite of her words, Jamie swung her legs back into the car and closed the door.

'There's a lot of chauvinism going around,' Josh pointed out drily, guiding the vehicle out of the parking lot and on to the main road.

'Especially in this car!'

'Of course, anything can be made palatable if presented properly,' he continued, ignoring her remark. 'The trick is to have all the facts, to be able to anticipate and counter any adverse publicity.'

'Adverse publicity?' The manner in which he had pronounced the words struck a note of apprehension within her.

'There's no delicate way of putting this,' he said acidly. From the hard set of his jaw, she sensed that had there been, he would not have used it. 'Tell me, Miss Kynter, if your picture appears in the magazine are we going to be inundated with young men who've had the pleasure of your company on the road?'

If the car had not been moving rapidly, she would have stepped out and never looked back no matter what kind of threats the man beside her might come up with. But as it was, she was trapped. 'How dare you!' she demanded bitterly, her stomach suddenly nauseous.

'Come now.' His tone was scornful. 'You know I have a basis for that question.'

'What happened . . . what happened between us . . . ,' she stumbled, unable to find the words.

'Yes, Miss Kynter? What did happen between us?'

'Nothing!' The word exploded from her, close to the level of a scream. It seemed to shock him, because he took his eyes from the road for a moment to look at her, then returned his attention to his driving as if to say he had considered her answer and chosen to disregard it. Taking several deep breaths, Jamic regained control and in a more level tone, enunciating each word distinctly, said, 'Nothing happened between us and you know it.'

'I'm not sure what I know. Why don't you simply answer my question? Have there been any one-night stands on the road which might be the basis for any adverse publicity?'

'No, none,' she seethed.

The car suddenly swung into the parking lot of a motel and she poised for flight, her heart catching in her throat at the sight of a long, streamlined Winnebago looming ahead. Parking in the vacant space next to the vehicle, he turned towards her. 'You wait here. I have a few items that belong to you. If you leave I'll return them to your uncle with a note of explanation, which's something I gather you would prefer to avoid, since you'd obviously chosen not to mention our . . . encounter to him.'

Pain, beating a tattoo at her temples, made it impossible to think. Unwilling to take a chance on what he might lead her uncle to believe, she sat stoically, too drained to care what happened next.

Climbing back into the car, Josh tossed a large paper bag into her lap. As she opened it, cautiously, as if it might contain a rattlesnake poised to strike, a strangled gasp issued from her throat. She did not remove the jeans, tee-shirt, and blue lace panties from the bag but simply crumpled it shut again, her knuckles white against the brown paper. 'Why didn't you toss them into the trash where you obviously believe I belong?'

'I don't know,' he muttered angrily. 'I really don't know.' Starting the engine, he backed the car out. 'Where is this house of yours? I did promise your uncle I'd take you there.'

Somehow Jamie managed to give intelligible directions. As they drove in the stiff stillness, a silence more deafening than a thousand drums, she sat looking straight ahead through eyes that refused to focus properly. She promised herself that once she left the confines of this car, she would never have anything to do with Mr Joshua Langley again. Not ever.

'I had the impression, this morning when you turned around from the window, that you expected to see me.' He broke the prolonged silence.

'I recognised your voice.'

'Are you certain that was the reason?' Here he hesitated as if the question was distasteful to him, then continued, 'Is it possible that you knew who I was before that?'

'No, I didn't know.' She wondered what target he was aiming for this time. Hadn't he already wounded her mortally?

Disregarding her answer, he said, 'It has occurred to me that you might have recognised me at the park and considered seduction as a method of gaining my co-operation.'

The words struck her like a physical blow. 'It was you who came to my tent, you who invited me into your camper,' she pointed out stoically in her defence, the fight drained from her.

'True. But it could have been a spur-of-the-moment decision. When you entered the camper, you were not sure how to handle the situation. But once inside, you decided it was too good a chance to pass up, so you played your little game. Only you hadn't considered all the aspects or repercussions of so rash an action. When the time came to . . . come through, you couldn't bring yourself to . . .' He let the sentence end itself.

'How would I have known who you were?' she countered, her throat dry, as she strained her eyes for a sight of the entrance to her driveway and an end to this nightmare.

'Your uncle could have warned you that I might show up and you could have recognised me from any number of pictures that appeared in the news media covering my acquisition of the magazine and the printing house.'

'My uncle didn't and I didn't.' Her voice sounded unusually quiet to her, almost abstracted, as if someone else was speaking. 'You were a total stranger to me.' A heavy silence followed, this time broken by Jamie as she added in a bland tone, 'It's your male ego, isn't it? I ran out on you when you thought you'd made a conquest, and you want revenge.'

Offering no response, Josh brought the car to a halt in front of her home. She climbed out without looking back at him. As she opened the front door, the tears began to roll in rivers down her cheeks and drip from her chin. Walking blindly through the house, she went into the kitchen and with shaking hands somehow managed to prise the lid from the aspirin bottle and swallow two of the white pills. Leaning on the sink, she sobbed violently, hoping the tears would cease but fearing they would flow for ever. How could he think such horrible things about her? Feeling the need to lie down, she released her grip on the counter and turned towards the door, only to discover Josh standing there watching her, his dark eyes filled with regret.

'I'm sorry, Jamie, but I had to know the answers. It was the only way I could deal with you, with . . .' He stopped abruptly as if he had already said too much. Tenderly, he pulled her into his arms, pressing her head gently against his shoulder. 'I had no right to be so cruel.'

She did not fight him. She let his warmth invade her senses, calming her, comforting her until the crying finally ceased.

He wiped the lingering wetness from her cheeks with his thumbs and handing her his handkerchief instructed her to blow her nose. Her hands were still shaky, but she managed.

It was then that the hiccups started. He ran a glass of water and made her take a drink and hold her breath. Suddenly, in the middle of this procedure, it dawned on her that he was treating her like a child. Blind, searing anger flared. First he had insinuated she was wanton depraved, and now he was treating her like a five-year-old who couldn't take care of herself! Swinging away from his touch, she glared at him. 'Get out of this house! Get out and leave me alone!'

For a moment he hesitated, then without a word acceded to her demand.

She stood staring at the now vacant spot he had occupied, remembering the warmth of his touch, the tenderness. Then the memory of his accusations burst forth anew and she ran from the room in an attempt to escape his lingering presence.

Out on the patio, she lay down on a chaise-longue, falling into the deep drugged sleep that accompanies emotional exhaustion, a sleep filled with dreams and images.

Awaking unrefreshed and groggy, she decided that positive action was the only solution. Upstairs she washed her face and changed into a pair of shorts with a matching top. Pushing Josh Langley to the back of her mind since she could not rid herself entirely of thoughts, some unprintable, concerning the man, she worked purposefully on her column until her uncle arrived home for dinner.

Sitting down at the table, Howard Kynter immediately launched into a tirade against what he termed the 'printing department' which had been the source of the problem at the magazine that day. Jamie could not supress a smile at the singlemindedness her uncle exhibited where *Meadow and Brook* was concerned. The 'printing department' was actually a thriving printing house with *Meadow and Brook* being only a small portion of its monthly output. Admittedly, the printing house had originally been started to print the magazine, but like an ambitious child had become prosperous and financially independent.

The story was that the originator of *Meadow and Brook*, a Mr Daniel Wells, had fought continuously with the hired printer over everything from the quality of the paper to the legibility of the copy. Then one month, owing to some mechanical problems, the printer had been a day late in producing the publication. Daniel had told the man that an imbecile could do better work, to which the printer had replied that Daniel possessed just the right level of mentality to prove that point. To the printer's disadvantage and Daniel's advantage, Daniel Wells had taken up the gauntlet.

Toying with the food on her plate while attempting to appear interested, Jamie listened to the blow-by-blow description of the battle which had ensued before a solution to the problem was finally worked out. All the while, she was bracing herself, like a man preparing to balance on a high wire in a strong wind, for him to ask how she and Josh had got along on the drive home. The question, however, never arose.

By the time the meal ended, she was tense and irritable, having steeled herself for what she considered the inevitable but which had not materialised. It was like waiting for the second shoe to drop and when it doesn't, the person waiting cannot relax because he is wondering why it did not fall. The need to get away from the strain Josh Langley's presence placed on her was great. As she and her uncle carried their coffee outside on to the patio, she said, 'I finished my column this afternoon and would appreciate it if you'd take it in tomorrow.'

'Be happy to,' Howard smiled at his niece, then picking up the evening paper began to peruse the headlines.

'Good,' she rushed on, 'because I'm planning to load the car up and get an early start. There are a couple of camping areas in the north-western part of the state I want to check out.'

'You know, I believe Josh Langley must be clairvoyant.' Howard lowered his paper to look at his niece.

'What do you mean by that?'

'When he dropped by this afternoon, he told me he would make his final decision concerning the O. C. Duckbill situation in the next few days and then he requested that you remain at home and not go off on another camping expedition until he'd spoken to you again.'

'He doesn't run my life!' Jamie's voice was hard with anger.

'Now, Jamie, the man isn't asking too much. You have plenty of material. The trip isn't necessary—at least, right at this moment. It wouldn't hurt for you to co-operate a little.'

'I don't like the idea of him giving you orders concerning my life!'

'It wasn't an order. It was more of a suggestion.'

'Joshua Langley wouldn't go out of his way to drop by the complex just to make a suggestion,' she persisted hotly.

'Actually, it wasn't out of his way. He had business in the printing department and stopped by to see me to let me know that he'd gotten you home safely. In fact, I was under the impression that the two of you had ironed out your differences?' There was a question in his tone.

Swallowing hard, Jamie avoided her uncle's eyes as she said in a more controlled voice, 'I guess I've been a bit edgy these last few days.' There was no way in the world that she was going to disclose to Howard what had transpired between herself and Josh Langley during that seemingly endless ride. Josh's visit to her uncle explained why there had been no inquisition at dinner. Apparently the man had anticipated this possibility and had headed it off. She could almost feel grateful to him, except that she knew he had only done it to save himself the embarrassment of explaining to Howard why he had felt it necessary to insult the man's niece in such a crass manner should Jamie have divulged the truth.

'So I've noticed. But now that you know Josh isn't such an ogre, I'm sure you'll begin to relax.'

Like a rabbit with a fox on its trail, she remarked to herself as her uncle returned to his paper.

CHAPTER THREE

Jamie awoke the next morning determined to put Josh Langley out of her mind, at least for this day. After seeing her uncle off to work, she spent an hour or so sketching illustrations for a book on fly tying she had been working on for the past year. Becoming restless, she put the book away and wandered down to the stream hidden beyond the line of trees at the far end of the back lawn. Her father and uncle had improvised on nature where this flowing water was concerned. The stream was not wide, barely eight feet across in most places and, originally, had been shallow along nearly all of its natural course through their property. After determining that the rest of its flow would not be affected in any drastic manner, they had arranged to have it dredged in spots creating deep holes in which stocked trout, both brown and rainbow, now resided.

Meeting the swift moving water at a shallow spot, she slipped off her shoes and waded out to a large boulder which protruded a good two feet above the water line. Seating herself on the flat surface, she drew her knees up under her chin and watched the five trout playing in a deep hole to her right. A large aged oak, whose exposed, intertwining roots created a delightfully intricate pattern, threw shadows over the water. She had come here often during the years in search of peace in times of turmoil, but today the serenity of this retreat did not prevail. She found herself glancing up at the trunk of the tree almost expecting to find Josh standing there, dressed in jeans and a shirt staring down on her.

'You're letting the man get to you,' she scolded herself aloud. 'It's not as though he has a death grip on your future.' This observation led her to a contemplation of a future elsewhere than between the covers of *Meadow and Brook*. The more she considered this possibility, the more self-reliant she began to feel. The series of articles she had been doing over the spring and summer, for instance, could be slanted a little more towards the recreational features other than fishing, such as swimming, boating, horseback riding, hiking or birdwatching which were available to campers at many of the parks she had visited. They would then be saleable to a more general publication. The material could even be used to compile a book for wilderness buffs on places to go and things to see.

Feeling much more confident about herself and her life, she walked back up to the house and made herself a sandwich which she carried out to the patio. There she discovered to her vexation that ridding her life of Josh Langley was not going to be easy. Picking up an old news magazine to thumb through while she ate, she found herself staring down at his photograph fronting a full-page article about him and his acquisition of *Meadow and Brook* and the adjoining printing house. Slamming the publication shut, she threw it back on to the table, only to retrieve it after a couple of minutes. 'To know your enemy is the only way to ensure his defeat,' she muttered as she began to read.

The writer portrayed Josh as one of the bright talents in the publishing world. Noting that at only thirty-four he had proved his abilities, the author cited examples of publications which had hired him during periods of financial crisis and which he had pulled out of their slump and back into fiscally solid positions.

Meadow and Brook, the article further elaborated, was the first time he had actually purchased a magazine. It went on to wish him luck, outraging Jamie by implying that the publication needed Josh's financial expertise to pull it out of dire straits and suggesting that he might have bought it only because it was part of the printing house package. She was honest enough, however, to admit that her outrage was more fear than anger. Her uncle had looked more worried than usual this past year and had, to her surprise, enthusiastically endorsed Josh Langley's take-over of the magazine. It was not a fear for herself but for Howard Kynter. For him the closing down of *Meadow and Brook* would be commensurate with the death of a child.

A deep frown furrowed her brow. Surely if the situation was as desperate as the article implied, she would have known. Howard had never once hinted at a problem of this magnitude, not of any magnitude. Choosing to believe that the implication of financial trouble had been added merely to give the story a note of drama, she read on.

Next the writer delved briefly into Josh's private life, mentioning his year-and-a-half-long marriage some eight years earlier to Selena Smythe, who was five years his senior and, at the present time, editor of one of the more popular women's monthlies. This information caught Jamie's attention since she found it difficult to think of Josh Langley as a frivolous man. A marriage of so short a duration seemed totally out of character. But then again, both parties involved were very success-orientated, and if neither was willing to give a little, their careers could have caused too great a conflict for the marriage to work.

'And knowing Mr Langley,' she mused aloud, 'he would have insisted that Selena do the giving!'

The ringing of the phone startled her. Dropping the magazine in the waste bin, she hurried inside to answer it. 'Your uncle asked me to call you,' Grace Adams' efficient voice came over the line, 'and tell you to defrost another steak. He's bringing Josh Langley home to dinner. And,' the woman added in a more confidential tone, 'if I were you, I'd make a special effort with the menu. Mr Langley strikes me as being a very interesting man. In my book, he's what any fisherwoman would call a "good catch".'

Ignoring Grace's editorial comments, Jamie thanked her for calling and hung up. For a moment she stood staring intently at the receiver as if trying to will it and the news it had carried out of existence. Then, with a resigned sigh, she walked slowly into the kitchen and took another steak out of the freezer. She had hoped for a longer reprieve. The man's accusations still burned in her ears and being civil to him was going to be difficult.

When the men arrived that evening, a few minutes before seven, she had ice in the ice bucket on the drinks cart, the salad chilling in the refrigerator, the charcoal heating in the barbecue pit, the ingredients for strawberry shortcake prepared and waiting to be put together at the last minute before serving, and herself dressed in a cool white cotton eyelet sundress with spaghetti straps.

'Sorry we're late,' Howard apologised, greeting her with a quick kiss on the cheek. 'The staff meeting ran longer than scheduled and then we stopped by Josh's motel so he could change.'

'I hope we didn't throw your dinner off schedule,' Josh added his apology.

'No.' Jamie forced a smile, intent on maintaining the pretence of being on friendly terms with him in front of her uncle.

'If you two will excuse me, I'm going to change into something more comfortable,' Howard announced, and was gone before the words were completely out of his mouth.

Jamie felt suddenly deserted. To her surprise, Josh too seemed uneasy. 'Can I get you a drink?' she offered with cold cordiality.

'Yes. A Bourbon on the rocks, please,' he replied, seating himself in one of the webbed chairs.

Even with her back towards him, she knew he was watching her. The hairs on her neck bristled and her hands shook slightly. Pouring herself a glass of white wine, she carried his drink over to him and sat down in a chair near-by. 'Have you been to Philadelphia yet?' she asked, her tone indicating that she was only making polite conversation and his answer was of little consequence to her.

'Yes. I found it very interesting. Philadelphia, the City of Brotherly Love—a very noble ideal.'

'But like all noble ideals, one finds it difficult to live up to such concepts under all conditions.'

A momentary flash of anger darkened his eyes. 'I apologised for the questions I felt obliged to ask you yesterday. They were necessary, both for your welfare and that of the magazine. A scandal wouldn't benefit either.' His tone was constrained, as if he was speaking to a difficult child who refused to listen to reason.

Jamie's cheeks flushed red with rage, but she made no response. She knew she had given him good reason to ask the questions by her wanton behaviour the night of the storm, but still she hated him for it.

'This land is very beautiful.' He spoke in a conversational tone, breaking the heavy stillness between them and making her feel like a child being coaxed out of a bothersome mood.

'My uncle and I like it,' she replied coolly. 'But I would have thought that you would prefer the bustle of city life.'

'No. As a matter of fact, I've been thinking about buying a place out this way myself.'

Jamie felt her composure slip. Having to accept the man as her new employer was bad enough, but to have him for a neighbour was unthinkable!

'I take it the idea doesn't appeal to you.' There was an angry edge to his voice.

'You may live wherever you wish. Certainly, my approval or disapproval would have no bearing on your decision.'

'A person likes to feel his neighbours are happy with his presence.'

'What's all this about neighbours?' demanded Howard, joining them.

'I was just telling Jamie that I'm considering purchasing a home in this area. I find it very much to my liking,' Josh explained, his tone once again casual.

'It's beautiful country,' Howard agreed, pouring himself a drink before finding a chair. 'You'll love it here. I understand the Stewards are planning to sell and move to Florida. Their property backs on to ours beyond that line of trees.' With a nod of his head he indicated the wooded area below them. 'But I'll bet my bottom dollar they miss the change of seasons. Sunshine the year round has got to be boring. I can't get into the Christmas spirit without, at the very least, a white dusting on the ground.'

'Perhaps you'd be willing to give me their phone number and I could check with them,' Josh requested.

'Be happy to.' Howard raised his glass in a salute towards his guest.

'Excuse me, I think the fire is hot enough for the steaks now.' Rising from her chair, Jamie escaped, leaving the two men to entertain one another. Returning for only a couple of minutes to place the meat on the grill and hand her uncle the turning fork, she again sought sanctuary in the kitchen, using the excuse that the salad needed her attention.

Back in her haven, she stood staring out of the window in an attitude of uneasy idleness. The table in the dining room was set and it was too early to toss the salad, but she was determined to avoid Josh Langley's company as much as possible. She berated herself for her cowardliness. It was ridiculous to allow the man's threats to buy a house nearby bother her. Even if they were neighbours, that did not mean she would have to see him any more often than she would be seeing him if he remained her employer. Still, the thought of his close proximity disturbed her.

'Howard sent me in to tell you he's turned the steaks and will be needing the platter momentarily,' a male voice cut into her thoughts, causing her to spin around guiltily to meet Josh's mocking expression.

It was obvious he had guessed that she was using the kitchen to hide from him, and once again she saw herself as a child in his eyes. She resented him for making her feel foolish and unsure.

Accepting the platter, he paused at the door. 'You do plan to join us for dinner?'

'Of course.' Her embarrassment turned to anger at the man's arrogance. 'But if you don't take that platter out to my uncle there won't be much worth eating!'

A derisive smile curling his lips, Josh rewarded her with a mock bow and left.

Quickly tossing the salad and pouring the glasses of iced tea, Jamie carried these out to the table, forcing a smile as the men entered from the patio with the meat.

'When we stopped by Josh's motel, he showed me through his camper,' said Howard as they began to eat. 'You should see it, Jamie. Even has a microwave oven!'

Smiling at her uncle, she fought the rush of colour which threatened to invade her cheeks as Josh's taunting dark eyes fell on her.

'Of course, it's much larger than anything you would need,' Howard continued, having missed the interplay between his niece and Josh Langley. 'One of those smaller vehicles about the size of a regular pick-up truck would be just right for you.'

'My tent suits me just fine.' With an effort, Jamie managed to keep her voice neutral.

'Except during storms,' Josh interjected, causing Howard to stop cutting his meat and look at his guest with a decidedly suspicious expression.

'I told Mr Langley . . .' Jamie began, only to be momentarily interrupted by Josh.

'Josh,' he corrected, and the edge in his tone cautioned her to obey if she wanted his continued co-operation in this little farce.

'I told Josh about my recent experience at Bennett Spring on our way here yesterday,' she lied, cutting a piece of meat as she spoke in order to avoid having to look either man in the face.

'That's just the kind of thing you could avoid with one of those self-contained recreational vehicles,' Howard commented. 'And Josh happened to mention that if you did purchase one it would be a business expense and therefore tax-deductible.'

'Josh seems to be full of little titbits of information!' Jamie threw a defiant look toward her protagonist.

'Your uncle is only thinking of your safety,' the object of her wrath pointed out. 'In fact, I won't be needing my vehicle for some time, and if you would care to borrow it for your next trip you're more than welcome to use it.'

'That's a marvellous idea!' Howard applauded the gesture, while Jamie smiled weakly.

Borrowing Josh's camper was out of the question. The memory of the events of Thursday night were strong enough without actually returning to the scene. A shiver shook her at the remembered awakening of passion. Embarrassed, she glanced up, to discover Josh watching her, a shuttered expression on his face.

'By the way,' Howard addressed Josh between bites, 'I spoke to Ray Harley about doing a series on the fisherman and the hunter in the ecological scheme of things and he's going to get to work on that right away. Jack Wells is going to handle the exposés.'

Jamie stared at her uncle increduously. It wasn't that they never ran articles on ecology or once in a while did an exposé, but he made it sound as if they were changing the entire format of the magazine from a hunting and fishing guide to a wilderness news journal. It wasn't a bad idea, she was simply puzzled by his easy acceptance of what were obviously Josh Langley's demands.

Howard Kynter had devoted his life to *Meadow and Brook* and she hated seeing him buckle under to a man who had probably never read one of their magazines cover to cover before he purchased the publication.

Before she made a comment she might regret, Jamie

hastily excused herself to return to the kitchen to put the desserts together. As she spooned freshly sliced strawberries over the scoops of vanilla ice cream atop slices of butter pound cake, she thought of several things she would like to tell Mr Joshua Langley. All of which were basically centred on her indignation at the way he felt he could come into people's lives and force them to do his bidding as if they were mere puppets and he the puppet-master.

The men were involved in a discussion of what type of exposés the magazine should pursue when she returned. In all fairness she had to admit, listening to the exchange, that Josh did listen to Howard's opinions. However, not willing to think well of the man, she pointed out to herself that he could afford to toss a few crumbs to her uncle since he had already won the main victory.

They adjourned to the living room with their coffee amid compliments from both men to Jamie concerning the dinner.

'It was really a very simple meal,' she said modestly. 'But I'm glad you enjoyed it.'

'The simple pleasures in life are always the most enjoyable,' Josh returned with a soft smile which immediately, although inexplicably, elicited a defensive reaction within her.

How would he know? she thought angrily. He married Selena Smythe, and from everything I've ever heard about the woman she could never be described as simple! Jamie's fingers came up to massage her forehead. Why had Selena Smythe come to mind? And why did she feel so hostile towards Josh Langley's past marriage?

'Do you have a headache?' Howard asked solicitously, noticing the gesture.

'No, I'm fine,' she assured him, hastily lowering her hand, then wished she had pleaded a headache. It would have been a convenient way of removing herself from Josh's presence.

'I'm glad you don't feel the need to leave us,' Josh remarked pointedly. 'Because I would like to discuss the future of the Duckbill column.'

It was the way he said it that really rankled her. Although he had used the word 'discuss', she knew he meant to tell her and her uncle what he had decided and expected them to agree to do his bidding with little or no argument.

'I've read through several years of the column, both when Jamie's father was doing the writing and after she had taken over. During the past three years I detected a definite change in the basic character of the articles, in the writing as well as in the message.' Jamie started to make a defensive comment, only to be silenced by Josh's raised hand. 'Let me finish.'

Condescendingly, she bit back her retort and, sitting rigidly, allowed him to continue.

'As I was saying, there's a definite change of flavour in the column. Jamie has added a touch of humor as if trying to tell the expert not to take himself so seriously; that fishing is supposed to be fun. Also, she has added travel information making the column more appealing to a wider range of people. All in all, I feel it's safe to say that she's made the column her own rather than a mere extension of her father's. Therefore I've come to the conclusion that the change in authorship should be made public. An alteration will have to be made in the heading—perhaps to "Fishing With Duckbill's Daughter". We don't want to drop the Duckbill because we need to capitalise on the association. However, the O. C. Duckbill byline will have to be changed. I think Jamie should use her real name.'

Jamie sat stunned. She had expected him to fire her or to allow the deception to continue. She had never seriously considered the possibility of coming out into the open, admitting authorship, and continuing the column under an altered heading and byline. Admittedly, he had hinted at this alternative yesterday, but she had honestly believed that he had asked those disgusting questions merely to harass her and let her know what he really thought of her. She had seriously misjudged him. In a very straightforward manner he had allowed her to put an end to any exposure before her uncle was made aware of behaviour on her part which might cause him discomfort. But still she could not forgive him for the cruelty of the accusations. It hurt too much to know that he could have believed her to be so promiscuous.

'Are you all right?' Josh was out of his chair and by her side before Howard had even noticed the sudden paleness of his niece's complexion.

'I'm fine.' She brushed his hand away from her cheek. 'I was simply shocked by your solution.'

'I don't know why you should be.' There was a cool edge to his voice as he reseated himself.

'You may be taking a chance with the readership,' Howard said dubiously. 'They could resent the deception, unless you plan to announce the change in authorship as a current event.'

'No, we'll go with the true story.' Josh's manner was firm. 'A lie would be too easy to discern and then they really would be angry. We'll play up the idea that Jamie continued the column as a personal memorial to her father. The public will buy that. Down deep, most people are sentimentalists.'

'You could be right,' Howard conceded.

'I don't see why my identity has to be made public,' Jamie broke into the conversation, her voice betraying her nervousness. 'I don't see why the column can't be allowed to continue as it is.'

'Because you can't have a career of your own hiding behind your father's image. Your uncle tells me you're working on a book. What name did you plan to publish it under?' Josh's tone was indulgent.

'My own.' The words came out hesitantly as she realised what he was leading to.

'And who will want to publish, much less purchase a

book by Jamie Kynter, an unknown?' This point made, he continued, 'Also *Meadow and Brook* can use the publicity.'

'I really don't see that my identity is all that big a news item,' she persisted.

'People love a bit of gossip, and this is precisely the kind of thing they find interesting for a short period of time. We'll use that period of time to make your name a household word.' Josh's tone was authoritative, convincing, and she did not doubt that he would accomplish what he set out to accomplish. She only wished she knew for certain exactly what he was striving towards. It was impossible for her to believe that if the magazine was in a financial crisis, the momentary publicity she would generate could save it.

'Our biggest problem at the moment is secrecy,' Josh was saying. 'We don't want this to come out as a slow leak and we don't want any other news source picking it up and killing it with indifferent coverage. The story will have to come out in the next issue.'

'Next month, you mean,' Howard clarified.

'No, this month.'

'It can be done,' Howard conceded, his mind already rearranging the current issue.

'Jamie will need to write an article about herself and her father stressing the closeness of their relationship and playing up the fact that he taught her all he knew about fishing. She must make the readers feel the devastation she felt at his sudden unexpected death and her need to keep his memory alive.' Josh elaborated. 'And as the new publisher, I'll do an insert editorial phrasing her unique talent and explaining that I felt it was only fair to her to allow her career to grow by making her authorship public.'

'Sounds solid,' Howard commented.

Jamie noticed the note of relief in his voice, as if her coming out into the open was a weight off his shoulders. This was an aspect of the deception she had never considered before. What if the truth had leaked out on its own without the support Josh Langley was going to give it? Thinking about it, she realised that her uncle could have been subjected to a deluge of accusations involving nepotism. Under different ownership, he might have lost his job or, at least, been made seriously uncomfortable for a period of time.

'We have to play this up big to produce the effect we want,' Josh was explaining. 'I want Jamie's picture on the cover.'

'Joe Marley would be the person to do the photography for that,' Howard proposed.

'I thought his speciality was wild life in its natural habitat,' Josh mused, catching Jamie's eye and causing her to flush slightly.

'Joe has been taking pictures of me since I was a baby,' she retorted defensively.

'Yes, he's an old family friend,' Howard interjected, looking confusedly from one to the other and wondering what he had missed.

'He'll have to be told why he's doing it.' Josh's tone was once again businesslike. 'Can he keep a confidence?'

'Absolutely,' Howard assured him.

'And about the background. We'll need a stream. I think we should go with a traditional fisherman—excuse me, fisherwoman—pose.'

'There's a stream beyond the trees at the back of the house,' Howard offered.

'Now wait a minute,' Jamie cut in. 'I really think this is going a bit too far.'

'If you were doing a major article on swordfishing,' Josh theorised, 'it would be only natural to have a fisherman displaying his freshly caught swordfish.'

'Am I to be the fisherman or the trophy?' she questioned sarcastically.

'Jamie, you know what Josh meant.' Howard's voice expressed his perplexity with his niece's manner.

Neither Josh nor Jamie noticed the man's reprimand. 'A man would be foolish to consider you anything less than a prize,' Josh replied, meeting the fiery green blaze of her eyes with a dark intensity so powerful as to cause her to turn away.

'Honestly,' she said in a more subdued tone, looking to her uncle for support, 'I really don't believe people are going to care who Jamie Kynter is or what she looks like.'

'There you're wrong.' Josh's manner was unshakeably resolute. 'With the right publicity hype, we can make people want to know all about Jamie Kynter.'

'I'm not so sure I want people to know all about me.' Jamie's expression was apprehensive. 'I've always led a very private life.'

'It won't last for ever,' he assured her. 'We'll work towards winding down the heavy publicity in around two months. By that time, you'll be known but not over-exposed. From then on we'll keep your name before the public in a more subliminal fashion.'

She flashed him a distrustful look but did not ask what he meant. A sense of alarm at the change her life was going to experience filled her. It was to be so drastic, so sudden. The desire to scream out in protest, to refuse to go along with his plans, was strong, but she held back. Her uncle wanted this and she owed him a great deal. Also, as much as she hated to admit it, Josh was right about her career. She might as well find out now, while she was still young enough to go into another line of work, if she could make it on her own abilities without her father's reputation to carry her.

'About the secrecy,' Howard was saying, 'I'll edit both the editorial insert and the article myself. I'll get Henry Balanio to do the cover once we have Joe's photograph in hand. He knows how to keep his mouth shut. If you two will get your material to me by Thursday, I can have the magazine ready to go to press by the weekend. That would be the best time for a covert printing.

'Other than absolutely essential personnel, the staff will not be told until Monday. We'll have a sort of coming out party first thing in the morning and give them each a copy then,' Josh added.

'Right,' Howard agreed.

'If you two men will excuse me—' Jamie rose from her chair unable to bear this conversation any longer, 'I'm going to clean up the dishes. All of this cloak and dagger stuff is a little too much for me!'

She was rinsing the dishes before putting them into the dishwasher when the kitchen door opened. Assuming it was her uncle coming to tell her that Josh had left, she did not turn to face the intruder but continued loading the machine. As she moved a wet dish from the sink towards its destination, the man who had entered spoke her name and the dish slipped uncontrollably from her hand to crash and break into tiny pieces on the floor.

'I'm sorry, I didn't mean to startle you.' There was a hard edge to Josh's voice that told Jamie he was more angry than sorry. Walking over to the corner, he grabbed the broom and dustpan standing there and began cleaning up the shattered china.

'I can do that,' she said tightly, but he ignored her as he swept up the last of the fragments and dumped them into the bin.

Returning the broom and dustpan to their places, he then turned his attention once more towards her. 'Your uncle is phoning Joe Marley to set up an appointment for your photographic session and I thought I would take this opportunity to reassure you that I will be here to support you one hundred per cent through this whole thing.'

'I'm perfectly capable of standing on my own two feet,' she returned sharply, unwilling to accept anything from this insolent man. If it wasn't for her uncle she would have refused to have anything to do with him at all.

'I'm sure you are.' Again his attitude was one of an indulgent father coaxing a petulant child. 'But everyone needs to lean on someone else once in a while. I simply wanted you to know I'd be around.'

'I have my uncle. I don't need nor want your help.'

'Some day you may change your mind,' he cautioned in a low, dangerous tone. His muscular form, clad in brown slacks and a brown pullover, reminded Jamie of a sleek wild cat as he came towards her. She cowered against the sink, knowing she should run for the door, yet unable to make her legs move.

Stopping when their bodies were within an inch of touching, Josh brought his hand up to stroke the line of her jaw with the tips of his fingers. His touch aroused emotions she was not willing to acknowledge.

As she started to edge away from him, his hands captured her upper arms, pinning her in front of him. She glared up at him, intending to demand that he release her. As the first word was being formed on her lips, his mouth found hers in a gentle lingering kiss.

Her rational side wanted to fight him, but her betraying body refused. She stood helpless against her own weakness with no will to push him away, yet a rock-hard determination not to respond.

As his mouth left her soft trembling lips, he stood back, holding her positioned in front of him as he searched her face. 'You're afraid of me and of your own femininity,' he mused in a quiet tone, as if seeing her clearly for the first time.

'No. No, I'm not,' she choked out defensively, holding herself under tight control. 'I'm simply not used to being roughly handled!'

'Roughly handled?' His mocking ebony eyes travelled to his hands resting lightly on her shoulders and then back to her face. Very slowly, allowing his fingertips to traverse the full length of her arms before relinquishing their featherlight contact, he lowered his hands to his sides.

'Get out!' she hissed through clenched teeth.

'As you wish,' he conceded, although his actions did

not comply with his words as his hand once again came up to contact her skin.

A tear of desperation escaped from the corner of her eye. She was not certain if she could hold out against another tender assault.

Brushing a loose strand of hair back behind her ear, Josh gazed hard into her face. His eyes had lost their darkness and were now a softly penetrating brown. 'Please, believe you have nothing to fear from me.'

As a second tear escaped, his lips brushed her gently and then he was gone.

The contact had been so light it was barely discernible, yet, as she watched the door close afer him, she could still feel the sensation of his mouth. It was as if a hot iron had touched her, burning its impression into her body and soul for ever.

'No! Never!' She addressed the emptiness adamantly, a grim expression on her countenance. 'I won't allow him to make a fool of me!'

She was placing the last dish in the dishwasher when the door opened anew. This time she turned to see who had entered her domain. To her relief, it was her uncle.

'Josh just left. He asked me to thank you again for the dinner.'

Jamie forced a smile as she started the machine.

'Joe will be here tomorrow morning, near seven-thirty.' There was a note of apology in Howard's voice. 'He said for this kind of assignment, he wanted to use the early morning sun.'

'Fine,' she agreed, somewhat reluctantly and definite-ly unenthusiastically.

'I wish we could have avoided all this.' Howard's demeanour was sympathetic as he approached his niece and placed a supportive arm around her shoulders. 'But sooner or later you were going to have to give up the Duckbill cover and strike out on your own.'

'Now you sound like Josh Langley,' she accused sullenly.

'Because in this instance he's right.' I've known for quite a while now that I had to find a way to get you out of this deception. But I couldn't come up with a plan that I thought would bring you into the open without possibly causing both of us irreparable harm or wouldn't have placed you in the position of having to start from scratch to build a reputation you've already earned.'

There was a tired look around her uncle's eyes and Jamie felt guilty for picking on him when it was actually her irrational susceptibility to Josh Langley which was making her edgy and irritable. 'I know,' she admitted in a less hostile, more submissive tone. 'It's just that this is going to be such a drastic change. But don't you worry— I promise to co-operate. In fact, I'm going to go to bed right now and get a good night's sleep so Joe won't have to touch up any dark circles under my eyes!'

Upstairs in her room, however, she discovered her promise was not so easy to keep as she tossed and turned trying to find a comfortable position while attempting to force Josh Langley out of her thoughts. Why did he have to come into her life? She had been comfortable, secure in her world, and now that world was topsy-turvy and she was not nearly as certain as her uncle and Josh that she would be able to salvage even a vestige of this peaceful existence.

Admittedly, she knew her uncle was right. Sooner or later she would have had to come out from under the deception, but surely there was a less painful, a less tumultuous manner in which this could have been accomplished.

Obviously, Josh Langley had not wreaked enough revenge on her with his insults. It was going to require a trial by fire to appease his male ego.

CHAPTER FOUR

Joe Marley arrived at precisely seven-thirty dressed in his usual worn corduroy pants and a tee-shirt with the words 'HAVE CAMERA. WILL TRAVEL' imprinted across the front. Jamie had never been able to guess the man's age. For as long as she could remember, he had always looked the same. A full, nearly white beard and handlebar moustache hid most of his face while his thick white hair hung in waves almost to his shoulders. He had once confided to her that he disliked wearing it so long but felt that it was now part of his image and people would be disappointed if he cut it.

'We're not doing a fashion layout,' he commented, shaking his head at the cool blue and white sundress she had so carefully chosen. 'I want you dressed in what you normally wear when you're fishing.'

Disgruntled, Jamie left him drinking coffee with her uncle on the patio and went to change. She reappeared several minutes later in jeans and a cotton shirt.

'Now we're getting there.' Directing her to turn slowly in front of him, he looked her over carefully. 'The hair's wrong,' he frowned at the sleek, tight chignon into which she had fastened her black tresses. 'Pigtails would be more suitable, and you need just a touch of pancake make-up for those circles under your eyes.'

Jamie blushed slightly at the mention of the circles as she hurried off to do his bidding.

Returning to the patio a third time, she demanded, 'Now how do I look?'

'Much too pretty to be spending all of your time luring fish,' Joe returned with an approving gleam in his eye. 'Now we're going to need some props. Run and fetch your fishing line, tackle box, net and whatever other paraphernalia you use. Oh, and don't forget that big straw hat.'

Casting him a dubious look, she hurried off to gather the requested items while her uncle helped him unload his gear and carry it down to the stream. Jamie joined them within minutes loaded down with fishing rods, tackle, waders, etc., and after giving her uncle a quick goodbye kiss, she and Joe went to work. He photographed her fishing in waders and out of waders, with her hat and without her hat. He snapped her tying on a lure, casting, catching a fish, netting the before-mentioned fish, holding fish up in the typical fisherman pose with waders and without waders. For three hours he continued to shoot her, sometimes posing her and other times having her move around naturally until he caught a good angle.

'My stomach is beginning to growl,' she complained at last, not mentioning her aching muscles which were feeling the strain from holding difficult postures for several minutes at a time.

'We're almost finished,' he promised, never taking his eye away from the lens of the camera. 'I just want a few of you out on that rock.'

He was referring to the boulder she considered her special place, and a protest began to rise from within her. However, knowing the man's obstinacy and having a strong desire to be finished with this session, she swallowed the objection and obediently rolling up her pants legs, waded out to the flat familiar surface. For another half an hour she posed in an assortment of positions. Just when she thought she would scream if he gave her one more direction, he told her to relax. Drawing her knees up under her chin, she concentrated on watching the trout swimming in the hole nearby. When that did not help relieve the tenseness in her muscles, she closed her eyes and let the sound of the swift-moving water permeate her senses. By the time Joe called out to her to say that he had decided he had enough footage, she was beginning to feel much better. Wading back to shore, she offered to fix him lunch, but he declined.

'Got to get home and get these developed,' he explained as she helped him carry his equipment back to his car. 'Your uncle said he needs them by tomorrow morning at the latest, and your Mr Langley promised to pay a most exorbitant price for my services. I wouldn't want to disappoint him.'

'He's not my Mr Langley,' she shot back without thinking, then fervently wished she had let the remark slide by as Joe gave her a searching look.

Perhaps it was his artist's eye, but he had always been able to read her better than either her father or her uncle, and she tensed under his scrutiny. 'If you need someone to talk to, I'm available.'

'There's nothing to talk about,' she assured him, being careful not to make eye contact as she placed the last piece of equipment in the back of his car. Still without meeting his gaze, she added, 'I've got to get something to eat before I faint. See you later,' and hurried off towards the house.

The old photographer, a long-time student of human nature, watched her retreating back with a knowing gleam in his eye. 'So our little Jamie is finally emerging from her cocoon,' he mused, then with a sigh climbed into his car and drove home to spend the rest of this beautiful day in his darkroom.

Jamie made herself a sandwich and carrying it out to the patio, stretched out on one of the lounge chairs to enjoy the warm sunshine. Exhausted from the unusual strain of being in front of a camera for four straight hours, she was beginning to doze off when an approaching male voice destroyed the transquillity of the quiet afternoon.

'How did the shooting go?' Sitting up, a startled expression on her face, she blinked several times to clear her vision as Josh seated himself in the shaded chair to her left. He was dressed in a business suit and his manner when asking the question was coolly official.

'What are you doing here?' Her voice held a note of alarm and she regretted not holding her tongue until she was fully cognizant.

'I seem to be making a habit of waking you,' he mused in a thoughtful tone, then in a more businesslike voice he said, 'I was at the Stewards' place to look the property over and thought I'd drop by to find out how the picture taking session had gone.'

'It went fine, I guess.' Jamie forced herself to sound calm while her heart was pounding with the remembered sensation of his lips. 'Joe took pictures for hours and I ache all over. I hope one of them is usable.'

'I'm sure one will be.' There was a hint of amusement in his voice that bothered her. She felt as if he was making fun of her. 'Is that what you wore?'

'We went for the Huckleberry Finn image,' she bantered to hide the uneasiness his inspection caused her, especially since the pigtails, the whole outfit actually, were so reminiscent of their first meeting. She could almost feel his hands again as they skilfully unbraided the wet strands of hair.

'Yes.' His tone was subdued. 'I think that was the way to go.' His eyes left her, wandering down towards the line of trees which hid the stream.

'My uncle isn't here. He's at the magazine.' She was uncomfortable in this man's presence and wished he would leave.

'I know. It's you I wanted to see.' He turned towards her again.

'Why? Did you forget some insult you wanted to deliver?' she snapped nervously.

'You certainly know how to carry a grudge. I thought we'd settled that issue.'

'What do you want?' His accusation had disturbed her and she tried to moderate her tone. She was not normally a hostile personality.

'I was hoping you and I could start all over again.'

'Start what all over again?' she questioned, distrustingly.

A smile began to curl the corners of his mouth but he quickly wiped it off and regaining the serious expression in which he had delivered the suggestion, said, 'Our relationship.'

'We don't have a relationship.' Her guard was up like a brick wall. She was not going to let this man penetrate her defences again.

'We have a business relationship,' he corrected. 'And in a few weeks we may be neighbours.'

'You're buying the Stewards' place?' The words came out sounding more like a reproach than a question.

'You don't approve?'

She schooled herself to present an indifferent front. 'It's a free country. A person can live wherever they wish.'

'But you would prefer that I didn't live so close.'

'Whatever your proximity, it won't affect me,' she assured him, while inwardly wishing he would leave the country or, even better, the continent. Then for some unexplainable reason she heard herself adding, 'Uncle Howard seems to think that you would make an ideal neighbour.'

An amused gleam shone in his dark eyes. 'With an endorsement like that, how could I refuse not to live here?'

Jamie flushed at her own duplicity. 'He doesn't know you as well as I do,' she shot back, more angry at herself than at the disturbing man who found her so laughable.

'And you,' he said, his voice deadly serious as he caught her chin and turned her face towards his penetrating gaze, 'don't know me half as well as you want to believe.'

A warning signal sounded in her brain. Unconsciously, her fear was mirrored in her eyes.

Rewarding her with an exasperated frown, he released her. Freed, she turned away from his disquieting contenance and concentrated on the line of trees in the distance.

'Getting back to my original question,' his voice was once again barren and businesslike, 'do you think we could start fresh and if not be friends, at least work together in a less hostile atmosphere?'

Taking a deep breath, she fought to clear her mind. The man had the most infuriating effect on her. However, they did have to work together for her uncle's sake, and to deny him this request would be childish and immature. 'All right,' she conceded.

'Good.' The word came out sharply as he rose to leave. 'Now that that's settled I'll be on my way. Have a good day, Jamie.'

Before her stunned mind could form a salutation he was gone, leaving her feeling strangely abandoned. She had expected some reaction other than total indifference to her capitulation. Shaking her head in an effort to clear the confusion of conflicting emotions the man's presence evoked, she told herself that he was impossible and not worth her consideration.

Forcing him out of her conscious mind, she spent the afternoon writing and rewriting the article about herself and her father. It was difficult putting words to her emotions, especially when she had to deal with the grief she had felt over his death. She made several unsuccessful attempts before her thoughts sorted themselves out enough to make sense on paper. It was a cathartic experience, but finally the article was written. It wasn't perfect. There were so many things she wanted to say about her father, but she could not find the correct words. However, the love she had felt towards him showed through, and that was, after all, what she had striven for.

Howard called around five to tell her not to cook dinner. 'Joe Marley will have the photographs from this morning's session ready by nine tonight,' he explained.

'So Josh has suggested that we pick you up and go to dinner and then go over to Joe's.'

'I really have a lot of polishing to do on my article before tomorrow morning,' she hedged. 'Besides, I'm much too selfconscious to choose a photograph of myself for a magazine cover. You men can handle that on your own, can't you?'

He spent a few more minutes trying to change her mind, but she steadfastly refused to accompany them, and he did not insist.

Relieved that she would not have to face Josh Langley again so soon, she retyped her article and after a light dinner watched some television before going to bed. That night she dreamt she was a little girl again. Her father was with her and they were sitting on a river bank talking. She had just escaped being bitten by a snake and her cheeks were still wet from her tears.

'You must learn not to panic,' he was explaining in a firm yet soothing tone. 'Fear is your worst enemy. It blocks your mind and clouds your common sense.'

Jamie awoke wishing she had learned that lesson better.

At breakfast, she handed her uncle the finished article with confidence. He, in turn, handed her the photograph the men had chosen the night before to front the magazine. It was the most traditional of all the poses, showing her standing in the the water in waders, her pole bent in response to the fighting fish that leaped from the stream a few feet away in his frantic bid for freedom.

'Very appropriate,' she said with a nervous laugh.

'Precisely.' He grinned broadly. 'I'm beginning to feel better and better about this all the time.'

I'm glad one of us is, Jamie thought, but kept the remark to herself. The reality of the photograph had set her nerves on edge again. The next few days promised to be interminable. Feeling the need to escape almost as desperately as the fish in the picture, she said, 'I would appreciate it if you would let me know by this afternoon if my article is okay. If Mr Josh Langley has no objection I want to take a little camping trip.'

'Do you want to borrow his camper?' Howard recalled the offer.

'No. I want to use my tent.' The set of her jaw told her uncle that no amount of discussion would dissuade her.

'I'm sure the trip will be fine as long as you're back for the Monday morning announcement session.'

Jamie paled. She had put that little piece of this gauntlet Josh Langley had laid out for her completely out of her mind.

'Now there's nothing for you to worry about,' Howard assured her, noticing her pallor. 'The staff at the magazine is like family.'

'But even in a family all the members don't necessarily get along,' she pointed out with a worried expression. 'And you have staff writers who've worked for *Meadow and Brook* almost since I was in diapers who are bound to be upset at my having a regular column while they have to fight monthly for their work to appear.'

He did not contradict her. Ray Harley had already expressed this concern when he had been informed of the identity of the Duckbill column's newest author. 'Dissent could be strong for a while,' he had warned bluntly, 'and you're bound to face accusations of nepotism.' The two men had worked together for years and Howard could always rely on Ray to be straightforward. 'However,' Ray had added with a smile, 'I think Jamie will make a lovely addition to our staff.'

Replacing his coffee cup in its saucer, Howard looked up into his niece's concerned face. 'I don't want you to worry about the staff. I admit that there might be a few unhappy feelings, but they'll pass. Remember, you have the owner's backing.'

This last remark brought a deep frown to Jamie's face. Lately her whole future seemed to hinge on Josh Langley, and she didn't like it one little bit.

'Wipe that frown off your face and pack your car,'

Howard directed. 'I'll read your article right now so you can be on your way whenever it suits you.'

She obeyed before he had a chance to change his mind. As she finished loading her equipment into the station wagon, he came out of the house with a pleased grin on his face. Assuring her that the column was wonderful, he told her to run along and have a good time.

Driving to a camping area in the Poconos which she and her father had visited many times, Jamie pitched her tent and spent the next three days fishing, hiking and generally enjoying the tranquil beauty of the mountains. When she returned home on Sunday, she was feeling less anxious, although certainly not relaxed about her unveiling.

Monday morning she dressed carefully, choosing a pale green sundress with shoes and bag to match and tying her hair neatly back into a chignon. Howard tried unsuccessfully to hide his nervousness. Neither was hungry, and after a breakfast of coffee and orange juice they arrived at the office half an hour before starting time. Grace was already there, arranging coffee cups, plates, napkins and forks on a long white cloth-covered table which housed a huge cake decorated with an icing picture obviously copied from the photograph used for the cover of the magazine and the words 'Welcome, Jamie' across the top.

'This was Mr Langley's idea,' the secretary explained before the question had been asked. 'He says if you have to do something difficult you might as well do it in style.'

Before Jamie or her uncle had a chance to comment, the door at the far end of the room opened and George Collins entered pushing a trolley with a large box strapped on to it. 'Congratulations, Jamie,' he called out across the room. 'You look terrific. Best cover this magazine has ever had!'

'Thank you, George,' she smiled as the man approached.

George Collins had supervised the actual printing of *Meadow and Brook* for as long as Jamie could remember. His acceptance made her a little less tense. Maybe she had been overreacting.

'Picked these up myself,' he said as he came to a stop and began unfastening the box. 'Didn't want any nosey-parker leaking out the word before the time was right.' Leaving the box by the table, he started back towards the door pulling the trolley. 'Be back for a piece of that cake,' he called over his shoulder.

'If the rest of the staff are as enthusiastic as George, we're in for some smooth sailing,' Grace remarked, but the tone in her voice told Jamie that the older woman expected some dissension.

Howard extracted three copies of the magazine from the box. Giving one to each of the women and keeping one for himself, he led them into his private office. 'I want to give the others a chance to assemble before I have to answer questions,' he explained.

Inside, they each opened their copies and looked over the lead article. 'You're very photogenic,' Grace approved, addressing Jamie. 'If Duckbill's Daughter doesn't work out you could always go into modelling.'

'Not on a bet,' Jamie responded goodhumouredly. 'My muscles were sore for two days after that session with Joe!'

'It does look good,' Howard smiled. 'And the piece you wrote about you and your father is excellent. I hope you don't mind that I included several family photos I had of the two of you.'

Jamie glanced through the pictures her uncle had chosen and approved. They brought back many happy memories.

As noises from beyond the door signalled the beginning arrival of the staff, Grace excused herself to direct the incoming personnel to the coffee and away from

Howard's office until he was ready to make an appearance.

Meanwhile, Jamie read Josh's insert. He praised her abilities without overdoing it. Grudgingly, she had to admit that the insert was well done. 'Probably Uncle Howard's editing,' she muttered.

'What did you say?' Howard looked up from his desk where he sat perusing his copy of the magazine.

'Nothing,' she responded quickly, wandering over to the window to watch a squirrel scampering from tree to tree. The minutes dragged by as she paced around the office, unable to sit down or relax.

Finally Howard glanced at his watch and pushing back his chair said, 'I think it's about time.' Pressing the button on his intercom, he spoke to Grace. Ascertaining that the staff was now fully assembled, he returned his attention to Jamie. 'Ready?'

'Ready as I ever will be,' she confirmed, while mentally noting Josh Langley's absence. Well, so much for his assurance that he would be standing by my side through all of this, she thought caustically. Bracing herself, she followed her uncle into the main room.

Howard clinked on a glass for attention and within seconds the private conversations which had filled the room with clatter ceased and all eyes were directed towards the man and his niece. 'I have what is for me a happy announcement and one that has been a long time in coming,' he began. 'But to talk about today and the future I have to first speak about the past. As all of you are aware, Duckbill has been a long-standing column in our publication. During the fifties and sixties and into the early seventies, the author of this column also produced numerous books on various aspects of fishing throughout the North American continent. Although he was not a public figure, preferring to keep his identity a private matter, he was accepted as an authority in his field. I use the past tense because in 1977, he died in a plane crash. It was a terrible blow to our magazine but even more to me personally. The founder of the column was my brother, James Kynter, Jamie's father.

'Jamie had travelled extensively with her father and had, under his tutelage, written several of his columns at various times. He had taught her everything he knew about fishing. They had been as close as any parent and child could possibly hope to be and his death came as an almost unbearable blow to her. In an attempt to help my niece through this difficult time, I convinced her to continue writing under her father's byline, keeping it, and with it his memory, alive. Thus, for the last five years, Old Duckbill has been Jamie Kynter.

'She has done an excellent job, adding her own dimension to the column, and now Mr Langley and I feel it's time for her to be recognised as the source. We've gone one step further by changing the heading on the column to one that's more appropriate for its authoress. It will now be titled 'Fishing With Duckbill's Daughter'. Now, I would like to officially welcome my niece to our staff.'

Someone started the applause—Jamie suspected it was Grace—and the others followed. Some responded out of shock, others because of a friendly feeling they had towards this girl they had known for so many years and others because they felt it was expected. The box of magazines was opened and distributed.

As she started to cut the first slice of cake, Jamie was beginning to breathe a little easier when Sara Lane's voice cut across the hushed whispers accompanying the staff's scrutiny of the cover and inside article. 'My goodness, that means Jamie must have been writing under that byline when she was only nineteen!'

An uneasy silence filled the room, only to broken by a male voice Jamie would have recognised anywhere. 'And as the new owner of *Meadow and Brook*,' Josh said as he moved towards her, 'I must say that to have people as talented as Miss Kynter working for me is a real pleasure.'

Grace took over the cake cutting, freeing Jamie to

accept the congratulations of the staff. Josh's presence by her side was an incentive for each and every one of them to offer her their support, and they did, though in some cases she sensed hostility. About the time the strain of smiling and exchanging stilted formalities with people she had bantered with for years was becoming too great for her to handle, an arm circled her shoulders.

'I think it's time I took you home and allowed these people to get back to work,' said Josh. Her uncle seconded the motion. Willing to accept help from the Devil himself, in order to escape from that room full of people, Jamie quickly retrieved her purse and walked out of the gathering on Josh's arm.

'You looked surprised to see me,' he commented as he guided his car out of the parking lot.

'I didn't think you were coming.' She shifted uncomfortably, wishing she had had the presence of mind to drive herself in this morning instead of riding with her uncle. Then she could have parted company with him outside the building rather than feeling forced to accept his offer of a lift home.

'I told you I'd be by your side through all of this.'

'I know what you told me. I just don't know you well enough to know when or if to believe you.' The open honesty of her words shocked Jamie.

'Now that you've admitted what the problem with our relationship is, I think it's time to rectify the situation. What we need is some time to get to know one another as individuals and not as the owner of a magazine and one of his columnists. Who knows, you might discover that I'm not such a bad sort after all.'

The thought of getting to know Josh Langley better caused Jamie strong feelings of trepidation. The man had a disquieting effect on her, and much as she disliked him she could not erase the fact that for a brief time on a stormy night she had come very near to willing knowing him intimately.

'I'll tell you what,' he continued. 'We'll take a holiday

for the rest of today and drive to Chadds Ford. I've been wanting to see the Brandywine River Museum. A friend told me that the building is as much a work of art as the paintings hanging inside. Is that true?'

'I honestly can't say,' Jamie admitted. 'I haven't been there myself. I guess I'm like the New Yorker who's never been to see the Statue of Liberty. You know it's there and figure some day you'll get around to seeing it.'

'Then it's time you saw it.' They had come to a crossroads and Josh turned the car west.

Panic swept over her. 'I would really rather go home and rest. This morning was trying.'

'If you go home you'll only sit around worrying about the effect this month's issue of *Meadow and Brook* is going to have on your career. Believe me, it will all work out just fine, and I'm sure the change of scenery will do you good.' His manner was firm.

'Really . . .' she began to protest again.

'Most employees humour their bosses to some extent,' he interrupted. 'Now why don't you humour me for today and try to enjoy yourself? I promise I'll act the perfect gentleman.'

'Act is the operative word,' she muttered under her breath as she settled back in her seat, accepting the inevitable.

An abundance of wildflowers, tall Black-eyed Susans with their ebony puffball centres and bright yellow-orange petals, tiny white Queen Anne's lace and a small variety of bush sunflower lined the split rail fence bordering the parking lot of the museum.

'What is the Brandywine Conservancy?' he asked, bringing the car to a halt. 'I noticed the sign read "Brandywine Conservancy and Brandywine River Museum"?'

'The Conservancy is a non-profit-making organisation of citizens intent on preserving the natural beauty of the Brandywine River and the surrounding area,' she explained. 'It's a conservation effort that encompasses not only the land but historical sites and customs as well in an attempt to preserve the total heritage of this region.'

'And the museum is part of the Conservancy?'

'Yes. You could say it's a functioning representation of the organisation's simultaneous interests in history, art and the natural environment. The building which is now the museum was originally a grist mill built in the mid-1800s. When the Conservancy took the place over they hired an architect out of Baltimore, James R. Grieves, to design a museum that would retain as much of the original structure as possible while showing off the Brandywine River which runs behind the building to its best advantage.'

'For a place you've never seen before, you certainly know a great deal about its history,' Josh remarked with a grin as they walked towards the tall three-storey, red brick structure. Rough wooden planks shuttered the windows on the side facing them, creating a primitive brick and wood motif.

'The Conservancy is of interest to me as an environmentalist,' Jamie replied.

Approaching the entrance, they passed gardens of cultivated wildflowers indigenous to the region. Presiding over this colourful display stood a statue of a young man with one hand gloved to safely provide a perch for a hawk while the other held two resting doves. The sculptor, Charles Parks, had named the work 'Boy With Hawk'.

Crossing a cobblestone courtyard, they entered the building. Inside the lobby areas on each floor were red brick. The elevator and stairs were enclosed in a huge white plaster cylinder forming a central core, while a crescent-shaped opening around a portion of this cylinder allowed sunlight from the skylight on the third floor to filter down to the main lobby. Retaining the circular motif, a curved three-storey wall of glass fronted the narrow tree-lined lawn separating the museum from the Brandywine River. The exhibit rooms were constructed with low beamed ceilings, white plaster walls and plank floors. There was a warmth, a harmony, about the building which pleased Jamie and gave her the impression that she was standing within a gigantic glass, brick, plaster, and wood sculpture.

The majority of the works on display in the museum were those of American artists who had been the top illustrators of their day and had learned their craft in the Brandywine Valley under the tutelage of Howard Pyle.

As they wandered from room to room, she found herself relaxing and actually enjoying Josh's company. They discovered a mutual fascination with the black and white oil paintings of the artist-teacher Howard Pyle and in the striking scenes created by N. C. Wyeth for the book *Treasure Island*.

On the third floor they paused in the crescent-shaped lobby to stand gazing out through the treetops on to the river below. The lawn was barely twenty feet wide and that, combined with the height from which they viewed the scene below, produced the sensation of being almost directly over the water. Josh's hand came up to rest companionably on Jamie's shoulder and she had to fight the urge to move closer to his sturdy frame. A warmth spread through her, muddling her thoughts.

Cautiously she turned her head to look up towards his face, only to discover that he appeared to be miles away, lost in thought. She shifted uncomfortably, resentful that her presence had so little effect on him while his created so many confused emotions within her.

Her movement attracted his attention. Indicating a group of young people peacefully floating down the river in large black inner tubes, he asked, 'And what exactly are they doing?'

'It's called "tubing",' she replied, moving away from his touch on the pretext of getting a better view. 'They float from one designated spot to another where friends pick them up.'

'Looks like fun. Maybe one day we could try that,' he suggested.

She found it hard to picture the man beside her floating lazily down a river, which caused her response of, 'Maybe,' to come out sounding doubtful.

A frown darkened his features momentarily before being replaced by a more neutral expression. 'I think it's time we had some lunch,' he said, leading her out of the museum and to the car without further comment.

He chose a restaurant not far from Chadds Ford. Over the meal they discussed the museums, the river and the paintings they had particularly liked, keeping the conversation impersonal thereby avoiding their usual conflicts. Much to her distress, Jamie felt more and more drawn to the man. His smile, when it reached his eyes, turning them to a soft mink, struck a chord deep within her. Towards the end of the meal, her eyes fell on his hands and she recalled how masterfully those strong fingers had massaged her tense back in the dimly lit camper. A shudder shook her and she quickly turned her mind away from this dangerous avenue of reminiscences.

'Are you cold?' There was a curious note in his voice. The restaurant was air-conditioned, but by no stretch of the imagination could it be termed chilly.

'No,' she responded in some confusion, concentrating on her dessert which had suddenly lost its appeal, afraid to meet his gaze.

Again a frown flicked across his features, and although it did not linger, the softness in his eyes vanished. The waitress returned with their check and gave him one more bright smile, making it obvious she found him more than mildly attractive. As they walked back to the car, he asked, 'Where would you like to go now?'

'Home,' Jamie replied, a surprised quality in her voice as she glanced at her watch to discover how late into the day she had dallied. 'I should be there when Uncle

Howard arrives. I have a feeling that today was probably not too easy for him either.'

'You're right.' Accompanying her to the passenger side of the car, he unlocked the door. 'Though I have to admit that I'm sorry to see the end of our little excursion. I've enjoyed your company very much today.'

'I've enjoyed today, too.' She smiled openly into his face for the first time since they had met.

The warmth returned to his eyes and for a moment she thought he was going to kiss her. Then a shuttered look clouded his countenance and he opened the door instead. Furious with herself for feeling disappointed, Jamie slid into her seat and stared straight ahead, while telling herself that she should be happy they had finally settled into a friendly yet impersonal relationship. But her traitorous mind kept veering off to picture another type of relationship.

They drove in silence for a while—not the relaxed, companionable silence one would have expected following the congenial atmosphere of the lunch but a stilted uncomfortable silence as though a barrier hung between them. 'Jamie,' Josh said at last, his tone apologetic, causing her to wonder embarrassedly if he had guessed the thoughts running through her mind and was now going to try to find some way of telling her how sweet he thought she was but that sweet wasn't his type, 'I hope you understand that today was only the beginning.'

'The beginning?' The words were what she had hoped to hear, but the tone was wrong.

'Yes. If my calculations are correct, you should begin to receive requests from other publications for interviews as soon as this month's issue hits the stands.'

Her jaw tightened as she realised how very foolish she had been once again where this man was concerned. She had allowed herself to begin thinking in personal terms when he only wanted an impersonal working relationship with, perhaps, a little uninvolved sex on the side. He glanced towards her and feeling the need to say something to cover her mortification she asked, 'What kind of interviews and why?'

'To the feminist magazine supporters you'll stand for a woman who made it in one of the sacrosanct corners of the men's world. To the others your story should be of high human interest—a daughter who loved her father so dearly she wanted to build a continuing memorial to him.'

'What about the deception which allowed me to enter this sacrosanct corner of the men's world, as you put it, or the accusations of nepotism my uncle will probably have to face?' she snapped back bitterly, her hurt coming out in an attack.

'We'll steer clear of those subjects and concentrate only on the positive aspects. I realise this is distressing to you, but remember I'll be by your side through all of it.'

Jamie sat back scowling. She didn't want him as a nursemaid. She could take care of herself.

'I hated to ruin our day this way,' he frowned. 'But I was afraid you hadn't considered the repercussions following your coming out into the open, and apparently I was correct.'

She sat silently, her only comfort being in the fact that he blamed her reticence on an anger aimed at the idea of being faced with unexpected interviews and not a humiliation directed at herself for being a fool.

As they drove up to the house, Howard Kynter came out to greet them. 'I was beginning to wonder what had happened to the two of you.'

'We drove to Chadds Ford,' Josh explained, 'I thought Janie could use a change of scenery.'

Forcing a smile, Jamie slipped an arm around her uncle's waist. 'You're home early,' she said as they walked towards the house.

'Thought I could use a break, too,' he said. 'And how was Chadds Ford?'

'Fine, just fine.'

Detecting a note of depression, in spite of her attempt to hide her feelings, Howard shot her a quizzical look.

'I'm afraid I spoiled the afternoon by mentioning the possibilities of interviews with other publications,' Josh said, noticing his concerned glance towards his niece.

'I'm sorry about all of this, honey,' Howard gave Jamie a hug as they went into the house.

'I've been more worried about you than the interviews,' she told him honestly.

'About me?'

'Well, I am your niece and, no other editor would have given a nineteen-year-old girl a byline.'

'True. Not even me, under normal conditions, and if you had no talent we could both worry. But I took a gamble and it paid off. You're even better than your father at knowing what the public wants to read about. Sure, there may be a few behind-the-back mutterings about nepotism, but they'll never amount to anything, because no one can deny your talent.'

'I hope so,' she sighed.

'I know so,' he assured her, then turning his attention to Josh who had followed them into the house asked, 'Can I get you a drink?'

'No. I have to be leaving. I just wanted to be certain everything went smoothly today.'

'The mailings went out this afternoon and the first news-stands will have their copies early tomorrow morning. We should know by noon if the other news media and publications are going to pick it up and give us a publicity boost.'

From the expectancy in her uncle's voice, Jamie could tell that he was as anxious as Josh for the plan to pay off to the fullest extent. In his case she could not fault him for this radical breach of her privacy. Howard Kynter, unlike Josh Langley who was in this merely for the money, loved the magazine as though it were a living, breathing being.

The phone interrupted Josh's response. Excusing her-

self, she walked out into the entrance hall to answer
it.

'Am I speaking to Miss Jamie Kynter?' the woman on
the other end of the line enquired in a curiously amused
tone.

'Yes, this is Jamie Kynter,' she replied dubiously.

'Miss Kynter, this is Selena Smythe,' the caller informed her, the tone indicating that Jamie should be
honoured by the notice of so important a personage.

'Selena Smythe?' Jamie repeated the name as if needing verification.

'Yes, Miss Kynter, and my magazine would like to do
an article about you.'

'An article? But why?'

'Unless my source has played a very elaborate practical joke on me, you are Duckbill's Daughter, aren't
you?' The woman's tone suggested that if a practical
joke had been played on her, the perpetrator would only
be safe if he or she left the country.

'Yes, I am,' Jamie admitted, a slight note of panic in
her voice. 'I didn't expect the news to be out so fast.'

'My dear,' Selena's manner was patronising, 'there's
very little that happens in the publishing world where my
husband—excuse me, former husband—is concerned
that I don't know about before the fait accompli.'

'I see.' The woman's mention of her marriage had an
unsettling effect on Jamie, producing a coolness in her
tone which caused her to sound much more composed
than she felt. 'And you want an interview?'

'Tomorrow if possible.' Selena was suddenly all business.

'Tomorrow will be fine,' Jamie agreed, forcing herself
to face the inevitable.

'Good. I'll send one of my staff to do the interview—
and a photographer, of course. You don't mind pictures?'

'No, I don't mind,' Jamie lied.

'My people can be at your home around nine in the

morning—unless you would rather come to New York.'

'Here will be fine.'

'And I'll be coming too.' A hint of sarcasm crept into Selena's voice. 'I'm curious to meet Josh's newest Eliza Doolittle. His Pygmalion complex has always intrigued me. Of course, I'm not complaining. I wouldn't be where I am today if it weren't for him, and I'm sure he'll do the same for you.'

Jamie's facial muscles tightened into a grim expression as the implication of the woman's words sunk in. An anger towards the man grew rapidly into volcanic proportions. This was all a game to him. He made a habit of playing with other people's lives, and she was his latest victim. Thinking back over the day, she saw it in a new light. He had functioned as a trainer, getting his man, or in this case his woman, ready to face what was to come next. She was a puppet to him, someone he could manipulate with little or no trouble. Promising herself that Mr Josh Langley would not have things his own way much longer, she bade Selena goodbye and hung up.

'What did she say to you?' Josh's angry tones startled her. She had not heard him join her in the hall.

'She asked for an interview tomorrow morning at nine and I agreed. Since you were obviously eavesdropping, you must know that.'

'That's not what I'm talking about. She said something to you about me, didn't she?'

'What could she possible say about you that would have you so worried?' Jamie's voice was acid.

'Nothing that was the truth. But then the truth was never one of Selena's strong points.'

'Truth is sometimes a matter of perception. Since you were obviously on your way out, I won't keep you. Goodnight, Mr Langley.'

For a moment he held her trapped in his dark gaze and even her anger could not free her, then abruptly he turned and left. Slumping back against the wall, she berated herself for allowing him to affect her so strongly.

'Jamie, who was that on the phone?' Howard called out from the living room.

Taking a couple of deep breaths to restore her equilibrium, she rejoined him. 'It was Selena Smythe. She and two of her staff are coming tomorrow for an interview.'

'I've never met her, but I have it on the best authority that she's a truly beautiful woman. I recall Paul Hallan saying he'd never seen anything on this earth to compare with her. I guess he meant it, because he married her.'

'She was married to Paul Hallan, the publisher?' Jamie frowned, then chided herself for even being interested.

'He married her a few years after her divorce from Josh. Gave her the editorship and fifty-one per cent of the voting stock in that magazine of hers as a wedding present. No one knows what happened, but the marriage didn't last long. He was quite a bit older than her. I admit I'm tempted to hang around and see if she lives up to her reputation,' Howard mused.

'You may if you wish.' Her uncle's remarks regarding the woman's beauty caused a harsh edge in what should have been a light response.

'You're not worried about the interview, are you?' he questioned solicitously.

'No—I'm just tired. I think I'll fix a quick dinner and go to bed. How does salad, cheese and cold roast beef sound to you?'

'Sounds fine,' he agreed, then added, 'And don't you worry—everything is going to work out just fine. Josh is with us one hundred per cent, and when the man who holds the purse strings is with you, you've got it made.'

And he certainly enjoys pulling those strings and watching us dance, Jamie thought bitterly to herself as she left the room to prepare their meal.

CHAPTER FIVE

Selena Smythe arrived the next morning in a cloud of expensive perfume and the very latest in Paris fashions, from the small pillbox hat perched jauntily on top of her naturally blonde shoulder-length hair to the tips of her scarlet toenails. Her expertly made up face accented her enormous liquid blue eyes, while her more than average height added a quality of willowy grace to her slender figure and Jamie was forced to admit that the rumours were correct. Ms Smythe was a strikingly beautiful woman. Next to this cosmopolitan beauty, Duckbill's Daughter felt suddenly very country and plain in her off-the-rack sundress and plaited ponytail.

Selena sensed the feeling of inadequacy in the dark-haired younger woman. In fact, she had counted on this reaction. 'Miss Kynter, do you mind if I call you Jamie?—and you must call me Selena.' Extending her gloved hand in a feathery light handshake, she hurried on before Jamie could respond. 'I'm so pleased we could have this little chat, although as I mentioned on the phone, I'm only here as an observer. Ms Hines,' Selena paused to indicate a frizzy redheaded, too slender young woman wearing enormous round-lensed glasses who was busily gathering equipment out of the car, 'will be the person doing the actual interview. I simply couldn't resist the opportunity to meet Josh's latest protégée. I can see he had a great deal of work cut out for him—but then he always did enjoy a challenge.'

Jamie, whose hairs on the back of her neck had bristled at being referred to as Josh Langley's protégée, was about to explain to Ms Smythe that she was no one's protégée except perhaps her father's or her uncle's when the sound of another car arriving stopped her. Looking up the drive, she recognised the blue Stingray coming towards them as belonging to the man she was about to deny, and the anger she had felt last night blazed anew. He had no right showing up here. His presence would only add credence to Selena's misconception of the situation.

'Now who could that be?' the blonde questioned accusingly. 'You didn't promise two interviews at the same time, did you?'

'No,' Jamie replied tightly, her response going unheeded as the driver emerged from the car, claiming all of the other woman's attention.

'It's Josh!' Selena's eyes were bright with anticipation. The look on her face reminded Jamie of a cat who had unexpectedly come across a most agreeable quarry.

'Good morning, ladies,' he greeted them, his manner more businesslike than friendly.

'It's so good to see you again, Josh.' As Selena spoke she took a step closer to the newest arrival and kissed him on the cheek. Remaining with her hands on his shoulders, she looked into his face and breathing an exaggerated sigh of regret, purred in a throaty voice, 'I swear you're getting handsomer and handsomer. Men always age so well. Sometimes I'm absolutely certain it was a mistake to end our marriage. We made quite a team.'

'We were never a team.' A frown flickered over his features, only to be immediately replaced by a coolly polite smile. 'Besides, independence must appeal to you. You look ravishing!'

'I don't believe I've ever received a more agreeable put off,' she laughed, sliding her hands in a caressing movement down the front of his jacket. Briefly, her fingers rested suggestively on the top button of his vest before completely dissolving the contact.

An icy chill swept over Jamie as she watched this intimate play. The desire to run inside and lock the door, closing these people out of her life for ever was strong, but she stood her ground. Her father had taught her never to run unless she knew exactly what she was running from and where she was running to. Admittedly it was a lesson she had found difficult and sometimes impossible to obey where Josh Langley was concerned, but today she was determined to maintain a tight control over herself.

'Good morning, Miss Kynter,' Josh turned his attention towards the silent dark-haired female, his eyes warning her to play his game. 'I thought that since this was your first interview I would sit in on the session for moral support.'

'I would have thought that after all of her years of experience in journalism that Jamie could handle a simple interview alone,' Selena commented, unable to keep a slightly biting edge out of her voice.

'Miss Kynter is a columnist, not a celebrity. She's used to doing the writing, not being written about,' he pointed out evenly, his mouth curved into a smile which did not reach his eyes. 'Besides, I'm only here as an observer, not a participant. Surely you don't object to that?'

'So am I, only an observer,' Selena placed her hand on Josh's arm. 'Therefore, I suggest you and I observe together and participate in a little interview of our own. We could discuss the good times we had. You might even find that they outweigh the bad.'

'Miss Kynter has a busy schedule. I suggest you line your people up and get started.' Josh spoke with an air of authority, bringing an abrupt halt to any further bantering for the moment.

'Of course,' Selena replied, a pout on her lips and fire in her eyes. 'You always did insist on business first.'

She's too successful to interest him—the thought flashed through Jamie's mind like a bolt of lightning. He's bored with her because she's past the point where he can manipulate her career.

'And since you've brought a photographer along, I

think the patio would be the best place to conduct the interview,' he directed. 'The out-of-doors background will be more in keeping with Miss Kynter's image. Don't you agree, Miss Kynter?'

'Whatever you say, Mr Langley,' she returned rigidly, then deciding it was time she took control, added, 'I'll bring out some iced tea. You can show these people where to go.'

As Selena moved towards her associates and began double checking to make certain they had not forgotten any necessary equipment, Josh touched Jamie's arm lightly, delaying her departure into the house. 'Be careful,' he warned as she shot him a hostile glance. 'Selena's a barracuda. Don't give her any ammunition to use against you.'

'And why would she want to use anything against me?' she hissed back contemptuously.

'Because you work for me for one thing and because she knows what sells magazines. A little tarnishing of your wholesome girl-next-door image would make good copy.'

'I would think working for you would be in my favour, since she appears interested in currying yours.'

'Not something you would do, is it, Jamie? Curry my favour?'

'No, Mr Langley—not something I would do.' She met his gaze defiantly, recalling an earlier allegation from him along this very line, among other assorted insults.

His eyes darkened as if he had followed her train of thought. 'I know.' The sincerity in his tone shook her. 'Just keep my warning in mind,' he cautioned once again as Selena approached.

'You seem to be upsetting Jamie,' the blonde remarked in an amused tone.

'You always said I was a difficult person to get along with.' A cold smile curled his lips.

'True.' Selena admitted, then with a mischievous

gleam in her eyes, she added, 'But I've decided to give you another chance.'

'Excuse me,' Jamie interjected, not willing to remain to hear Josh's reply. Turning quickly away from the pair, she hurried towards the house, her mouth pressed into a tight line.

Joining the others on the patio a few minutes later she discovered that Josh had again been choreographing the setting. He had arranged for the redheaded interviewer to sit at the round umbrella-shaded table, explaining that she would need a place to put her recorder since she was planning to tape the session. He had then positioned Jamie's chair so that her back was to the line of trees towards the end of the lawn. This provided a woodsy backdrop for any pictures that might be taken during the interview.

'I'm Jerry Sloan,' the photographer, a middle-aged, clean-shaven, fatherly type, introduced himself as Jamie finished serving the drinks and started to seat herself. 'Do you mind if I take a couple of pictures with you standing in front of that Oak before we start?'

'Of course not,' she agreed graciously, throwing Josh a look, daring him to make any suggestions, only to discover that he had seated himself and Selena out of the way in a shaded spot and was extracting a folder from his briefcase. Apparently, he felt he had done what he could to promote the success of the interview and was now planning to turn his mind to other business. The look in Selena's eyes expressed her displeasure towards this latest development. She's a fool to care about the man, Jamie thought scornfully. I, on the other hand, am too smart to fall for such an arrogant, self-centred boor.

After several photographs, Jerry Sloan thanked her and reseating himself, affected a nonchalant attitude, as if his job was now complete. However, having known Joe Marley all of her life, she was careful to note that the man retained his camera in his hand and had positioned himself in the most advantageous spot for taking candid shots during the interview. He was a real pro, she cautioned herself. He would sit, feigning indifference, encouraging her to relax her guard and then when she least expected it, sometime during the interview when she allowed an emotion to emerge, he would quickly snap the picture capturing the moment on film for exposure to the world.

With sudden insight, she saw herself as the fish and the questions to be asked by the interviewer as the fancy lures. It was Josh Langley's influence, she frowned. However, she did attempt to maintain an air of restraint and schooled herself to think before she answered.

'I'm Barbara Hines,' the redhead introduced herself with a friendly smile and a handshake. 'And I'm so pleased to meet you, Miss Kynter.'

'Please, call me Jamie.' This was said with a nervous smile.

'And you must call me Barbara. Do you mind if I record our conversation? That way I can be certain of accuracy in any quotes I might want to use.'

'No, of course not,' Jamie agreed, while inwardly filled with a desire to destroy the small black machine.

Rewarding her with a final encouraging smile, Barbara switched on her recorder and referring to her list of questions said, 'Let's start at the beginning. Could you tell me something about your childhood? What memories are the most vivid?'

'I guess the most vivid, certainly the happiest, are the times I spent with my father travelling around the country camping and fishing. He was almost continuously on the move.'

'You had no permanent home?' The interviewer interjected a note of sympathy into her voice.

'This place has always been my home,' Jamie explained, keeping her tone level and non-defensive. 'My father and uncle purchased this house jointly following my mother's death and I lived here with Uncle Howard during my school terms. My life was not unsettled, just full.'

'But still, it must have been difficult without a mother,' Barbara persisted.

'My uncle and father were enough family for any child.'

'They were strict?' The question was asked with a coaxing smile.

'They cared a lot and tried to make up for my not having a mother,' Jamie fielded the question, unwilling to go into details about her private life.

'Would you say you had a happy childhood?'

'Yes, there was always something going on. It was an active, exciting life. I guess you could say that my father treated me more like a son than a daughter, taking me with him whenever it was feasible and teaching me everything he knew about fishing.'

'And about writing, according to your article in this month's issue of *Meadow and Brook*,' Barbara added.

'Yes, by the time I was in my early teens, he had me typing his copy and then after a while he taught me how to edit. When I was sixteen, he started letting me write a column once in a while. When the check would come for the work, he would deposit it in my name. "For your future," he would say.'

'And what did you envisage as your future?'

'I don't know. I suppose at the time I thought of the writing as more of a game than a career. Like most girls that age, I pictured myself married with a home and children. Although I recall once thinking of becoming a pilot. I remember we were in Canada flying around from one lake to another and the pilot of the little bush plane let me take the wheel.' A sadness came into Jamie's eyes as this memory sparked a more painful recollection.

'Your father died in a plane crash in Canada, didn't he?' The interviewer picked up on her mood.

'Yes. I was to have gone with him, but I was ill,' she responded absently, wishing for the umpteenth time that

James Kynter could be beside her to help her through this ordeal and protect her from . . . Josh Langley?

'That was lucky for you,' Barbara mused, then frowned at herself for making what could be interpreted as a callous statement.

'I'm sorry, I didn't hear what you said,' Jamie apologised, shaking her head slightly as she glanced surreptitiously towards the man who kept impinging on her thoughts in a most disturbing manner.

'Never mind—it wasn't important. Tell me how you and your uncle hit on the idea of continuing your father's byline.'

'I was very depressed following my father's death and my uncle saw that as a way to help me.'

'I understand,' the redhead smiled encouragingly, 'but what I want to know is exactly what happened.'

'I see.' Jamie allowed her mind to carry her back to those dark days. 'I was in college at the time and I tried to continue my studies, but I couldn't seem to concentrate. My uncle brought me home and I wandered around this house for weeks trying to get my life back on some track or another, but I just seemed to be drifting. Then one day he came home and told me to come into the den. He sat me down and announced that we had to have a talk. He explained that following my father's wishes, he'd never divulged his brother's identity as O. C. Duckbill and that since my father's death, he'd continued to run the column using material he had on file which had not yet been printed. You see, my father was a very practical man and always kept five months ahead in his writing. That way, if an idea for a book hit him he could devote several months in a row to it without worrying about his column. Anyway, my uncle explained that he'd continued the column so far but that that particular month's issue would be the last in which my father's byline would appear unless I wanted to do something about it.

'I asked him what he meant, and it was then that he

suggested I began to write the column, pointing out that I had already done this in the past. At first I refused to consider the idea. I was scared, afraid I couldn't do as good a job as my father. But Uncle Howard convinced me that he could help me through the first few months. Then, if either of us didn't feel comfortable about what we were doing, he would announce that owing to ill health Duckbill was retiring. I knew he missed my father terribly, too, and like me, he saw this as a way of keeping Daddy's memory alive. The continuation of the column would be a lasting memorial. I think, also, that he knew my father had planned on my following in his footsteps and one day taking over the column and felt that he should try to fulfil his brother's wish. Anyway, I agreed, and you know the rest.'

'Not exactly,' Barbara Hines corrected. 'I don't understand why you suddenly decided to stop this long-running memorial to your father and replace his byline with your own.'

Jamie hesitated, unsure of how to proceed. It sounded so crass to say that the time had come for her to have a career of her own, and besides, she had been happy remaining in her father's shadow.

'I felt it was time the public knew the truth,' Josh Langley interjected, startling the others present who had assumed he was so absorbed in his own work that he was paying no attention at all to how the interview was progressing. Laying down the papers he had been reading, he moved to stand behind Jamie's chair. 'When I bought the magazine, I had some promotional ideas centring on O. C. Duckbill. You can imagine my surprise to find that the author of the column was not the craggy, bushy-bearded old codger I'd envisaged but a very beautiful young woman.' Here he paused to smile down on Ms Hines, who was at once captivated. 'My first inclination was to let the situation ride and allow Jamie and her uncle to continue their very noble deception. However, the longer I thought about it, the more I felt that for two reasons we had to bring the truth out into the open. Firstly, I will admit I wanted to follow through on several of my original ideas. Secondly, and most importantly, I felt that Miss Kynter's talent should not go unrecognised. She's a gifted writer and an expert in her field.'

During Josh's explanation the photographer had sprung into action, snapping pictures of the columnist and her employer from all angles while Jamie kept a forced smile on her face and tried to look natural and relaxed with Josh Langley presiding over her like a lord and master.

'What are some of your promotional ideas?' Selena questioned, joining the trio and forcing the photographer to curb his activities.

Josh's hands moved from the back of Jamie's chair to her shoulders, the grip of his right hand tightening ever so slightly to let her know that he wanted no public protest from her. 'I'd planned to put out a line of fishing equipment and men's sportswear under the Duckbill label. Now, of course, it will be a line of women's sportswear. Also, I'd been considering a contest.'

'A contest? You mean like "guess how old Duckbill was when she landed her first . . . fish . . . and win a trip to Yellowstone?' Selena's tone was caustic.

Jamie reddened at the implication in the blonde's pause before and after the word "fish", but a hardening of the pressure of Josh's hand on her shoulders kept her quiet.

'I was thinking more of a fishing contest among a few well chosen experts,' he responded mildly, giving no indication that he had caught the tasteless hint in Selena's remark.

'And do you plan to go ahead with the plans for this contest?' Ms Hines queried.

'Possibly. Although, I may have trouble finding contestants. The male experts might be afraid that the fish will jump into Miss Kynter's net simply to be caught by such a beauty.' Josh's tone was warmly amusing as he concentrated his full attention on the redheaded interviewer.

Ms Hines laughed in a friendly, captivated manner, completely charmed by the dark-eyed Mr Langley.

'And if the fish can't be influenced by Miss Kynter's beauty' (the word 'beauty' being pronounced in an acrimoniously suggestive manner) 'perhaps the other contestants could,' Selena purred.

Josh's jaw hardened as he turned his attention towards the blonde. 'I suggest we return to our positions as observers and allow Ms Hines to finish her interview.' Without waiting for Selena to comply on her own, he took her arm in a none too gentle grip and led her back to the seats they had so recently vacated.

'Jamie,' Barbara Hines addressed her interviewee once again, her eyes mirroring her disappointment in the loss of Josh's attention, 'how do you feel about these projects Mr Langley has outlined?'

'I have to admit that this is the first time I've heard of these particular plans,' Jamie began hesitantly, then recalling the warning pressure of Josh's hands and not wanting to cause her uncle any grief, she added in a more positive vein, 'but they do sound interesting.'

Leaning towards her interviewee, Ms Hines said in a whispered aside, 'I would think anything to do with Mr Langley would be more than interesting!'

Jamie could think of no response, being unwilling to make any statement which could be taken as an endorsement or denouncement.

The redhead, however, was paying no heed to the woman to whom she had just spoken, having glanced over Jamie's shoulder to be rewarded by a smile from Josh.

'Barbara,' Selena's voice was harsh on the quiet country air, 'I think you should finish. It's nearly eleven and we don't want to keep Jamie from her busy schedule.'

'Yes, Selena,' Barbara responded hastily, returning

her attention to the notebook in front of her. 'Now let me see where I was. Oh, yes. Jamie, how does it feel to have not only crossed over into one of the last remaining bastions of male dominance but to be considered an expert by others in the field at such a young age?'

'I don't feel as if I have crossed any boundaries,' Jamie replied thoughtfully. 'Fishing has always been a part of my life.'

'But honestly, isn't one of the reasons you and your uncle chose to keep your identity a secret because you feared the male readership of *Meadow and Brook* would not happily accept advice from a woman?' Ms Hines persisted.

'We live in an enlightened age, Barbara,' Josh again interrupted, rescuing Jamie from making an uncomfortable confession. Then glancing at his watch, a slight frown wrinkling his brow, he added, 'And I must apologise, but it's late and Miss Kynter has a twelve-thirty appointment in Philadelphia.'

'I'm sure we have enough for our article,' Selena supported his suggestion to end the interview.

'I hope you'll be fair to Miss Kynter,' he remarked as Ms Hines and the photographer gathered up their equipment and prepared to leave.

'I don't know what would make you believe otherwise,' Selena returned innocently. 'I'm certain Barbara will be more than fair. In fact, she'll be kind. We women are always proud when one of our own makes it in a man's world.'

Jamie cringed at being referred to as 'one of our own': She would never willingly include herself in any group even vaguely associated with Selena Smythe.

'I'm glad to hear that,' Josh returned, surprising Jamie by the threatening note in his voice.

But what surprised her even more was the slight hint of nervousness in Selena's manner. 'If you don't trust me, we could have dinner and I could let you read the copy before it goes to press,' she suggested.

'I appreciate the offer, but there are people who might cry "foul". It would be best for all concerned if you run your article the way you see fit. I'll let you know if anything about it doesn't please me.'

'As you wish.' Selena took the refusal in her stride, as if she had expected it.

In the front of the house, while Jamie was exchanging salutations with the photographer and interviewer, Selena leaned close to Josh and remarked in a voice loud enough to carry to the dark-haired girl's ear, 'Getting up this morning early enough to make the drive here on time was a strain. You remember how much I love to lie in bed in the morning. But it was worth it to see you again.'

There was a suggestiveness in the woman's delivery which caused a twinge deep within Jamie. Obviously, whatever had happened to break up Selena's and Josh's marriage, Selena was willing to forgive and forget and begin again, and Jamie could not help wondering if Josh still harboured any feelings of affection towards the statuesque blonde. He must have loved her deeply once to have married her, and not only had he never remarried but, to Jamie's knowledge, his name had never seriously been linked with any other woman. Assuring herself that whatever happened between the two of them could make no difference to her, she attributed the hollow feeling in the pit of her stomach to hunger.

Before Selena's car was out of the driveway, Jamie started back towards the house. She had her head in the refrigerator trying to decide what would best suit her appetite when a male voice sounded from close behind her. 'I hope you have something in there that's good,' Josh remarked, looking over her shoulder. 'I'm famished!'

'I don't remember inviting you to lunch,' she said coldly.

'You can't expect me to drive you into Philadelphia on an empty stomach.'

'I don't expect you to drive me anywhere,' she threw over her shoulder, unable to turn around because of his close proximity.

'I told you we have an appointment this afternoon.'

His warm breath played havoc with her nerves while his nearness threatened her defences. Anger was her only salvation. 'You told Selena, Ms Hines, and the photographer, but you didn't tell me. I don't appreciate your high-handed ways, Mr Josh Langley—and don't expect me to bow and scrape to your every whim! If you want someone who'll fall at your feet, go get in your car and catch Selena.'

'Selena is a part of my past, a part I prefer to forget.' There was a harsh note of finality in his voice.

How easily he discards people, she thought hostilely, promising herself that she would never be one of his toss-aways.

'The roast beef looks good.' Reaching around her, he removed the platter from the refrigerator and carried it over to the counter. 'Do you have any mayonnaise and wholewheat bread?'

'Yes, to the mayonnaise,' she answered stiffly, relieved by his departure. 'But no wholewheat. You'll have to settle for white or rye.'

'Rye, then,' he stipulated. Finding a knife, he began slicing the meat. 'Do you want one sandwich or two?'

'None.' Her manner was curt. 'Josh Langley, you can't come in here directing my life as if I was a puppet on a string!'

'Look, I'm sorry I couldn't give you more notice.' He paused in his carving to face her, a note of apology in his voice. 'But I didn't have a definite appointment set up with Flavius until just before I came over this morning. The man is always on the move and no one knew for sure where he would be and when.'

'Flavius? The designer?' she questioned, interested in spite of herself.

'Yes, the designer. I want him to do the line of sportswear I mentioned.'

She practically threw the sandwich he had handed her on the counter. 'And that's another thing! Sportswear, fishing 'equipment', contests—you make me sound like a three-ring circus! Who do you think you are anyway, making all these plans without saying a word to me? Without even asking me if I want to be involved in these schemes of yours? Did it ever occur to you that I might not want to be rich and famous, that I might like my life the way it is?' Finishing this tirade, she swung around, intending to leave the room, but he caught her arm.

'Now that you have that out of your system,' he turned her around so that he could look directly into her face, 'I have a few things to say. Firstly, I apologise, if what I'm doing is upsetting this little Never-Never Land you've been living in, but when I bought the printing house, *Meadow and Brook* came as part of the deal. It was not a part I would have sought. The magazine is in deep financial trouble and is going to fold if its circulation isn't built up fast. Those of us who don't exist in little ivory towers know what a competitive world it is on the outside. Your uncle has done a respectable job over the years, but times have changed and he didn't change quite fast enough. The printing house has been carrying the magazine for the last two years. That can't go on. I'm trying to save it by altering the format. We're putting in more exposés, more environmental impact material, and you're the bait to draw in new readers.'

'I don't believe you.' Her words were brave, but the fear in her eyes told a different story.

'You can check the circulation figures.'

'It would kill Uncle Howard if the magazine went under.' Tears swelled up in her eyes. 'He's devoted his entire life to *Meadow and Brook*. It means everything to him.'

Josh's arms circled her, drawing her against him. 'Your uncle is a strong man. He'll survive no matter what happens,' he assured her in soft tones as he stroked her head gently. 'Besides, I honestly believe we can save the magazine.'

Tears overflowed running in tiny rivulets down her flushed cheeks. She did not push him away. She needed his assurances, his strength.

As they stood, the man and the woman, together in the stillness broken only by her gentle sobbing, the warmth radiating from his body penetrated her shock-cooled skin and a feeling of security and protectedness spread over her. His maleness permeated her senses. She could not deny the stirrings his touch awakened. Slowly, her hands moved upward to his shoulders as she lifted her face to him.

His lips met hers in a gentle probing kiss deepening into a possessive passion when she responded.

Entwining her fingers in his thick black hair, she moulded her body to him. The taut muscles of his thighs pressed against her soft contours, igniting a burning need, a longing. Her lips parted, allowing him full possession of her mouth, and with a groan of pleasure he accepted the invitation as his hands moved over the rounded curve of her hips.

Deserting her mouth, his lips played erotically over her face and neck. 'You taste salty,' he whispered, his breath tantalising on her sensitive skin.

Timidly she tasted his neck. The action pleased him, causing a satisfied laugh to issue from deep within his chest.

'I don't want to ever see you cry again.' His lips brushed sensually against her skin as he spoke. 'I promise I'll take care of you for ever.'

The words triggered a distressing series of thoughts, culminating in the image of Selena as Jamie wondered if he had made this same promise to the blonde. A shudder shook her, forcing her back to reality. Releasing her hold on him, she pushed against the granite wall of his chest with all the strength she could muster. Again he had so very easily elicited this wanton behaviour from her, and she was frightened. He had been right in assuming that she had, in many ways, been well protected, well insulated from the world. He had torn down her ivory tower and although she was not sure what would happen to her next, she was determined that he would not destroy her.

'What's wrong?' He relaxed his hold only slightly.

'I don't want you to take care of me, Josh Langley. I intend to take care of myself!' The words exploded from her.

'Jamie!' He spoke her name cautioningly. There was anger in his passion-darkened eyes.

A look of fear came over her face as she realised that he had brute strength on his side. She might have started something this time that could not be easily stopped. Her body began to quiver like that of a trapped animal.

Josh's expression became shuttered as he released her. 'You're right. A person has to learn to stand alone before they can stand with someone else. It's part of growing up.'

Jamie backed away from him, her sudden freedom almost as terrifying as his embrace.

'You'd better go and comb your hair and fix your lipstick,' he directed, resuming his sandwich making. 'We have to be going soon.'

As if he was a general and she a private, she spun around and without thinking, without feeling, did as he commanded.

It wasn't until she stood at the top of the stairs preparing to descend that she again began to function on her own accord, causing her to come to an abrupt halt. She could not face him. Not now. Not ever.

As her eyes travelled over the familiar surroundings in an effort to regain some form of equilibrium, they fell on a picture of her uncle. Recalling what Josh had said about *Meadow and Brook*, she knew she had to face him, for Howard Kynter's sake. Steeling herself with the thought that her uncle needed her help now just as she had needed his help when her father had died, she once again began to move, descending the stairs slowly.

'You look as if you're going to a funeral!' Josh's cynical voice sounded from the entrance to the living room. 'I believe the idea is that we're trying to prevent one.'

Spurred on by his contempt, Jamie squared her shoulders and marched resolutely down the last few steps.

'That's a brave little soldier,' he remarked drily, meeting her at the bottom of the stairs and handing her a glass of milk and a sandwich. 'You'll have to eat on the way.' Before she could protest, he rushed her out of the door and into the car.

She had no appetite, but eating the sandwich gave her something to occupy her attention while they drove and for that reason she nibbled away at it, finishing it by the time they arrived at their destination.

Meeting Flavius did a great deal to lighten her mood. The man was a short, wiry cyclone, never staying in one place, much less one room, for more than ten minutes at a time. He worked out of a huge warehouse of a building. They moved from room to room as he matched his sketches to various bolts of fabric. Generally she was pleased, even excited by his ideas. However, she did feel compelled to protest a scanty halter design matched with a pair of very abbreviated shorts.

'That outfit would be fine for sunbathing,' she argued. 'But if a person wore it on a river bank, she would either be bitten to death by insects or burned unmercifully by the sun or both.'

'Not to mention what a distraction it would be to the other fishermen!' Josh laughed, and was rewarded with a frown.

In the end, Flavius unhappily gave in and struck the design from the proposed collection. When he asked if she had any other comments, Jamie suggested a denim fishing vest to accompany the line of jeans he had proposed with fishing motifs embroidered on the pockets and in some cases around the hemlines and down the legs. Both men thought it was an excellent idea.

'I thought Miss Kynter could model some of the collection herself, especially for the store posters,' Josh said as the trio left the fabric rooms and walked back toward Flavius's office.

'She's a little too busty and round-hipped for my taste in models,' the man replied. 'No offence, Miss Kynter, but I prefer for my customers to appreciate the fashion rather than the soft curves below the fabric. However, you are very photogenic, as evidenced from your picture on the cover of the magazine, Josh showed me, and you're the name behind the label. Also, as a man I can appreciate how very becoming you must look in a pair of jeans, so I see no reason to object to Josh's suggestion. In fact, now that people know what you look like, I would say it's a necessity.'

Jamie was not certain whether she should be flattered or insulted, but taking her cue from the amused gleam in Josh's eyes, she accepted the man's statements politely, choosing to assume that all of his remarks were strictly business orientated.

During the drive home, Josh spoke only of matters relating to the magazine. He even refrained from making any remarks about Flavius's comments pertaining to her figure, keeping his manner friendly yet impersonal.

Jamie attempted to match his attitude, and while externally she was able to keep up the farce, internally she was a jumble of emotions. As hard as she tried, she could not keep her attention focused on his discussion of the sportswear line. The scene in the kitchen kept replaying itself through her mind, tormenting her. She could not deny that she had initiated the kiss, nor could she deny the hunger in her response to his touch. Humiliation at her behaviour caused a hard knot in her stomach. But what really hurt was his reaction when she had pulled away. He had been able to instantly turn off any emotions she had aroused within him. While she was standing there feeling torn and bruised, her whole being a mass of confusion and fear, he had lost interest in the entire episode and had returned to preparing his lunch as if nothing had happened.

She had to face the fact that to him she was a gimmick to sell his magazines and nothing more. Admittedly, he saw her as a reasonably attractive member of the female species and wouldn't mind taking her to bed. However, he wasn't interested enough to force himself on her. He had left it up to her to issue the invitation, and she was determined never to issue another.

By the time they came to a halt in front of her home, she felt drained both physically and mentally. When her uncle came out of the house to exchange a few words with Josh she hoped he would not invite the man to dinner. She had had all of Josh Langley's company she could stand in one day.

'Looks like we're making quite a splash this month, judging from all the phone calls I've received today,' Howard commented.

'All good, I hope.' There was a definite question in Josh's voice.

'Most were very positive.' Relief was evident on Howard's face. 'I also received four more requests for interviews with Jamie.'

'Set them all up in the next few days,' she requested. 'I need to go on another camping expedition. As I mentioned to you before, there are a couple of parks in the north-western part of this state I want to check out before the end of the summer. I don't want to get behind in my column.' Then giving her uncle a quick kiss on the cheek, she turned towards the houses.

Howard stared after her retreating back. Jamie was like her father in that she always kept several months ahead in her writing, so there was no real reason as far as the magazine was concerned for her to take this trip. However, he sensed her need to get away and was willing to yield. 'I hope we're not pushing her too hard,' he remarked to Josh, a look of concern on his face.

'She's got a lot of strength,' Josh assured him. 'She'll make it okay.'

'I have a feeling that she resents being pushed. I hope this doesn't lead to a lifetime feud between the two of you.'

'You and me both,' Josh admitted, his jaw set in a hard line. 'I'll drop off the contracts for the sportswear and the fishing equipment late tomorrow. See that she signs them before she leaves.'

CHAPTER SIX

Over the next couple of days Jamie retold her story until she felt like a broken record. Her smile was beginning to feel plastic and her weight was slipping. At the present rate of loss she figured she could qualify as one of Flavius's models by the end of the summer. She signed the contracts Josh had given to her uncle and declared herself free of the man, at least for a while.

It was with a silent prayer for a bit of solitude and relaxation that she threw the last of her fishing gear into the back of her car the following Wednesday morning and took off. Her life had been altered drastically in the past weeks and she needed some time to reorientate herself and adjust to the changes. What she was hoping to find on this expedition was some remnant of the peaceful existence she had experienced before Joshua Langley had barged into her world.

Driving north-west through the farmlands and into the mountainous region of the state, she tried to recapture the feeling of serenity this green forested land had always created within her in the past. But Josh Langley's image would not leave her alone. 'He and Selena belong together,' she told the trees. 'Well, they do!' she snapped at the dark-haired girl in the rear view mirror. 'He uses people and she doesn't mind being used. He might think he's using me right now, but I'm on to his game and I'll go along with it for Uncle Howard's sake, but as soon as the magazine is back on solid ground I'll happily part company with Mr Joshua Langley!' This pronouncement, which should have given her a great deal of satisfaction, did not. In anger at herself, she switched on the radio and forced her mind to concentrate on the music and the inane remarks made by the disc jockey.

The music and banter did help, and by the time she pulled into the campground she had selected for her first overnight stop the tenseness was beginning to leave her muscles. The air smelled sweet and fresh and a smile actually came to her lips as a warm summer breeze stirred a few wayward strands of hair.

However, she was soon to discover that this was simply the lull before the storm. Inside the combination general store and registration office, the heavy-set woman behind the counter was overly solicitous, and when Jamie handed in her completed form exclaimed loudly, 'I knew it! I knew it! You look exactly like your picture. It's a real pleasure to meet you, Miss Kynter.' The heads of several other occupants in the store turned in Jamie's direction as the woman came around the counter, blocking her exit. 'Could I ask you to do one little thing?' she continued, her voice still loud enough to carry distinctly throughout the small establishment. 'I know people would be so excited! If you could just autograph the copies of *Meadow and Brook* we have here on sale.'

Realising there was no polite way out of this request, Jamie forced a smile and asked dubiously, 'Where do you want me to sign?'

'Right on the front,' the woman responded quickly, her expression one of triumph.

'I want one of those,' a man coming up behind Jamie declared as she began to scribble her signature above the jumping fish.

'Me, too,' a female voice chimed in as a woman dressed in jeans and a sweat-shirt with a young child in tow rounded the corner of an aisle to join the group now gathering around the magazine rack.

For the first time since this whole business had begun, Jamie felt the real impact of being a celebrity. She was both scared and elated at the same time. Hard as it was for her to believe, these people wanted Jamie Kynter's autograph! With a slightly flushed face and an open smile she exchanged pleasantries and handshakes before leaving the building and, back in her car driving to her campsite, she had to admit that the attention had been fun.

However, what she hadn't considered was the undying interest people have concerning those few who, for one reason or another, become the centre of news. It was while she was hammering in the stakes to secure her tent that she received a taste of what was yet to come. A small child Jamie judged to be around six wandered over and stood watching her with the wide-eyed insistent stare only children feel free to use. She smiled up at him, then went on with the job of getting her campsite in order for the night. Finally, as if the question could not be contained any longer, he demanded, 'You really famous?'

Turning to face him, she said in a thoughtful tone, 'I've never thought of myself as famous.'

'My mom says you are. She says you know everything there is to know 'bout fishin'.'

'I wouldn't say I know all about fishing.'

'She says she saw your picture on the front of a magazine and you was catching one,' the child persisted.

'Tommy, you come back over here and leave Miss Kynter alone!' a woman's voice ordered from the campsite next door. Following this unheeded command, a short-haired brunette walked over and taking the boy by the hand said, 'I hope Tommy hasn't been a pest, Miss Kynter.'

'No,' Jamie assured her politely.

'Well, I'm real sorry if he has,' the mother apologised. Then dragging the protesting child along, she started back towards their own campsite. 'You mustn't bother people like Miss Kynter,' Jamie heard her reprimanding the boy. 'They need their privacy, too.'

This last remark was one Jamie was to remember as the evening progressed. It was after she had built a fire and seating herself comfortably in her lawn chair began to eat the sandwiches and fruit she had packed that she noticed people were watching her. At first she thought it must be her imagination, but when the same couple walked past her campsite for the fifth time she knew she was not mistaken. Glancing over her shoulder, she discovered Tommy's mother concentrating on her so intently that the dinner the woman was supposedly tending burned. Feeling more and more like the clown in the centre ring of a three-ring circus, she fortified herself with the thought that she was saving the magazine her uncle loved while at the same time promising herself that she would get even with Josh Langley if it took her the rest of her life.

But it was out on the stream the next day that she had the encounter she most dreaded. She was standing near a deep hole, very gently playing a fly across the top of the water, when an elderly fisherman approached. 'Thought I recognised you,' he said in a matter-of-fact tone. 'You're Jamie Kynter, Duckbill's daughter.'

'Yes,' she acknowledged, giving the man her best smile while attempting not to let the fly out of her control.

'Been reading that column for quite a while.' The man watched her play her line, a critical look in his experienced eyes. 'Noticed a change over the past few years, but I'm not saying it was for the worse.'

A short silence followed this statement as a fish moved to strike and Jamie expertly set her hook into the trout. The man watched her play the fish to shore, then, leaning down, netted it for her. Slipping the hook from the fish's mouth, he examined the minute fly. 'Tie your own, I see,' he nodded with approval. 'Guess you have to when you fish with unbarbed hooks most of the time.'

'Yes,' she replied politely, knowing that she was talking to a man who had fished close to three times as many years as she was old.

'You want this fish, or shall I let him go?'

'Let him go.'

Lowering the net into the water and holding the end secure, the man allowed the fish to regain its freedom. Then, rising, he extended his hand towards her. 'It's been a real pleasure to meet you, Miss Kynter,' he said as they shook hands.

Watching him walk away, Jamie experienced mingled feelings of elation and relief. If this man was representative of the readership of *Meadow and Brook* then she was going to be accepted. Her coming out into the open was going to work out all right, after all.

She stayed out for a little over three weeks and by the time she returned home, she was getting used to being recognised. She didn't feel totally comfortable with the situation yet, but she was adjusting.

'You look rested, but you've dropped a little too much weight,' Josh remarked as he joined her and her uncle on the patio the morning after her homecoming.

'Flavius seemed to think I was a bit on the plump side,' she pointed out as she poured the man a cup of coffee, wishing she had a touch of arsenic to flavour it with.

'I'm not interested in pleasing Flavius.'

'You're not interested in pleasing anyone but yourself, are you, Mr Langley?' she returned disdainfully.

'I assumed that since you'd stayed away for three weeks your trip had gone well. Apparently I was mistaken. Did you run into a critic or two or three?'

'No. People were very nice,' she confessed, almost resentfully.

'Then what is your problem?' he demanded in a voice a father might use with a petulant child.

'I don't enjoy being on display.' There was fire in her eyes as she met his gaze. 'I felt like a freak in a sideshow. People watched me all the time.'

'That's the price you have to pay when you're a luminary. You'll get used to it and learn to ignore it.'

His 'it's-nothing-to-get-upset-about' attitude irritated

her further. 'I'll never get used to it nor learn to ignore it.'

'Josh, I have to leave in a few minutes,' Howard broke into the hostile exchange, hoping to halt the confrontation before it reached warlike proportions. 'I thought we'd covered everything over the phone last night.'

'I forgot to ask you about Ray Harley's exposé series,' said Josh, taking a sip of his coffee.

'I received his first piece yesterday. It looks good. It's at my office, if you're interested in stopping by to read it over.'

'Maybe I'll drop by later.'

'It seems to me that a busy man like yourself who spends so much time arranging other peoples' lives would be more organised.' Jamie commented sarcastically. 'You could have saved yourself the trip out here if you'd simply asked Uncle Howard that question last night, or even called him this morning.'

'I do have to confess that seeing your uncle was not the main reason for my early morning arrival. Howard mentioned that you were back when I spoke to him yesterday, and it's you I've actually come to see. I didn't know you were so snippy in the morning or I would have waited until after your second cup of coffee,' he frowned.

'Then if that's the case,' Howard interjected, pushing back his chair and rising, 'I'll be on my way. I have a magazine to run.'

'Uncle!' Jamie's voice held a plea.

'Don't bite his head off,' Howard advised in a hushed whisper as he bent down to give his niece a kiss on the cheek. 'It's easier to work with a friend than an enemy.'

Forcing a smile and pleasant note into her voice, she wished him a good day and gave him a wink to indicate that she understood what he had told her. However, as soon as he was out of hearing range, she turned to the man who had so drastically altered her life and demanded, 'What is it you want of me now?'

110

'Flavius has finished putting together a show of the sportswear for the Duckbill label and I want you to do some publicity shots for the store posters. Also, I want you to arrange your schedule so that you're available for the show for the buyers. We want them to feel that the product is being enthusiastically supported by its namesake.'

'Well, it isn't,' she retorted. 'I can't think of anything that would thrill me less than having my name emblazoned across the rear ends of thousands of women.'

'What about the closing down of the magazine?' Josh offered coldly.

'I don't see what having a line of clothes with the Duckbill label is going to do for the circulation of *Meadow and Brook*,' Fear softened her anger.

'Any publicity you receive will rub off on to the magazine.' His manner was impatiently indulgent as if she should already understand this. 'Right now, Duckbill is synonymous with *Meadow and Brook* in the minds of the public.'

'When do you want me for the publicity photos, and when is the show?' Jamie capitulated with a grimace of displeasure.

'I'll call Flavius now. You'll have to go in for a fitting.' Jamie moved uncomfortably under his close scrutiny. 'You must have dropped a couple of sizes. I don't like it. You're going to have to take better care of yourself, because I don't have the time right now to play nursemaid.'

Before she could offer her less than flattering opinion of him as her nursemaid, he was gone through the French doors, leaving her glaring after him.

On his return he did not sit down but came to stand near her chair. 'I've spoken to Flavius and he'll make himself available to you this afternoon at two. Also, he wants to arrange the show for two weeks from today. I have to fly to Europe on business this afternoon and don't know when I'll be back, but I'm sure the two of you

can handle all the details. Grace has the invitations
ready to be printed except for the date and Flavius
knows who should receive them.'

'Yes, Master,' she muttered.

Josh's brown-black eyes met the jade green of her
anger. 'Maybe I should stick around for the publicity
shooting,' he mused. 'I don't believe I've ever seen a
more beautiful pair of eyes as when you're angry with me
or when . . .' He stopped himself from completing the
sentence, but she knew what he was thinking and an
indignant quiver shook her chin. 'I have to be going. I'm
glad you survived your first public exposure so well,' he
said, changing the direction of the conversation. Then
with a note of bitterness, he added, 'I wouldn't have
wanted to fly off to Europe without one of our little spats
to see me on my way!'

Jamie started to make a sharp retort when her throat
suddenly contracted in fear. Her father had flown off
and never came back. She wanted to be rid of Josh, but
not that way. The thought that he might be harmed filled
her with an unfathomable dread.

'Have a good day,' he threw over his shoulder as he
walked away from her. 'I feel certain that the news of my
imminent departure has brightened your outlook considerably.'

'Josh.' His name came out shakily.

Pausing, he looked back at her questioningly, a hard
frown etched into his features.

Fighting to keep her voice level, she said, 'Have a safe
trip.'

As if he could read her mind, his expression softened.
'I promise I'll try to get back in time for the show if you
promise not to lose any more weight.'

She nodded, not feeling confident enough to speak.

'That's a good girl!' Returning to where she sat, he
placed a fatherly kiss on her cheek, then departed.

Jamie sat alone looking out over the green lawn to the
trees beyond. Angry tears trickled down her cheeks. She

already had a father figure in the form of her uncle and she neither needed nor wanted Josh Langley to fill that capacity. 'I don't want him in any capacity,' she announced defiantly to the empty air, wiping away the offending streams of water with the back of her hand.

That afternoon when she went in for her appointment with Flavius, the designer was delighted with her weight loss and quickly made arrangements to have her fitted with several outfits. On her way home she stopped by her uncle's office to give Grace the time and date she and Flavius had chosen for the show. The woman promised to have the invitations printed and hand delivered to the designer by the next afternoon. 'Mr Langley said they were to have top priority,' she explained when Jamie shot her a questioning look. 'In fact,' she added with a twinkle in her eye, 'he seems to give everything connected with you a high priority.'

'That's just because I'm his newest experiment in running other people's lives,' Jamie frowned.

'You're being a little hard on the man, aren't you?' the secretary commented.

'Maybe,' Jamie admitted, much to her own surprise.

The frenzy of activity in which she was involved over the next couple of weeks enabled her to push her dark-eyed antagonist to the back of her mind during her waking hours. He did, however, continue to haunt her dreams.

Three days of her time were spent posing in various outfits for the store posters which would be used to advertise the Duckbill line. To her delight, Joe Marley had agreed to do the shooting. The photographer had once told her that he considered fashion photography barely one step removed from pornography, and she could not help questioning him about his decision to agree to do these sessions with her.

'Firstly, I'm doing this because you're the model,' he told her. 'And secondly, Josh Langley offered me twice what I normally make for my top work, which is no little sum.' After a brief pause, he had added, 'The man is certainly going all out to see that you get what he considers the best!'

Jamie flushed slightly at the insinuation in Joe's voice, but she made no response. In all fairness, she had to admit that she was grateful to Josh in this instance. She did not enjoy being photographed in these circumstances, and if the photographer had been a stranger, she was not certain if she could have gone through with the sessions. 'Which is probably why he made sure Joe would take the pictures,' her cynical side pointed out.

The time passed swiftly and before she realised what was happening, it was the night before the show at which the line of fashions bearing the Duckbill label was to be presented to buyers from all over the country. Josh was not back, nor had he contacted her during his absence. He hadn't said he would, but she had assumed that he would call to check on how the details were going, since he had choreographed all the previous stages of her metamorphosis.

'It's not important whether he's here or not,' she told the emptiness of her bedroom as she lay in bed that night trying to find peace in sleep, her nerves tense with anxiety over the show less than twenty hours away.

'But he was here for my coming-out party and I'm a little superstitious,' she elaborated, attempting to justify the need she suddenly felt for his presence without admitting to herself that she missed him. In the next breath she chided herself angrily. 'Superstitions are for children.' With a tight fist she pounded her pillow into a more comfortable position. 'And besides, I certainly don't want to become dependent on Josh Langley's presence. The man is on his way out of my life for good, and I'll be happy to be rid of the arrogant, overbearing, imperious, dictatorial bore!'

'Arrogant, overbearing, imperious, and dictatorial; yes. But definitely not a bore,' her honest side corrected.

Frowning at herself, she pounded her pillow once

more and after tossing and turning, changing her position every minute or two, she finally fell into a fitful sleep—the last thought in her disharmonious mind being that he had shown up at the last minute for her coming-out party.

There was, however, no last-minute appearance by Josh Langley the following evening. In spite of Jamie's trepidation the show went well. She appeared on stage with Flavius several times during the presentation, each time wearing a different outfit.

In addition to the buyers, representatives from the fashion magazines and several general publications had also received invitations. Their photographers busily snapped pictures of the authoress and designer as well as the models. With luck some of these photographs would be used in articles providing free publicity for the new line.

The buyers bought sparingly, but Flavius explained that that was to be expected. That they bought at all was a good sign, he assured her.

Dutifully, she mingled with the buyers and magazine representatives following the presentation. About the time her exhausted mind was losing focus, a familiar voice brought her back sharply.

'Miss Kynter, I want to tell you how impressed I am,' Barbara Hines commented enthusiastically. 'I may even buy one of those fishing vests. I don't fish—can't stand the feel of the slippery things—but with all those pockets, I'd never have to carry a purse again!'

Jamie smiled at the remark and Jerry Sloan snapped her picture.

'Selena sent us, since I'd originally interviewed you. I don't usually cover fashion shows, but I have to admit I found this one to be a real kick,' Barbara rattled on. 'Are you going to be doing any television commercials to promote the line?'

'I hadn't considered that,' Jamie responded, a startled look in her eyes. 'I hadn't considered that at all.' Her stomach became very uncomfortable as she wondered if Josh had thought of this possibility. If this was the next step in his plans for her, she knew exactly what she was going to tell him to do with that little idea.

'Everyone's doing their own TV spots these days,' the redhead noted matter-of-factly.

'You'd be a sensation,' Jerry Sloan added. 'That black hair matched with those green eyes is a photographer's dream.'

'Thank you,' Jamie smiled nervously.

'Selena would have come herself,' Barbara re-entered the conversation, 'but she's in Europe.'

Jamie felt as if she had received a physical blow; however, she managed not to show any reaction. So Selena was what was keeping Josh so very busy! As soon as Barbara and Jerry left in search of refreshments, she sought out her uncle and, after congratulating Flavius once more, departed.

'I've always been proud of you,' said Howard as they drove home, 'but tonight I finally realised that you've grown into a very capable young woman. Josh was right.'

'Right about what?' she asked tightly, the mention of his name bringing out even more strongly the feeling of desertion she was experiencing.

'He said you'd be just fine, that you'd do an excellent job.'

'I'm glad he was so confident,' she said drily.

'The man knows talent when he sees it.'

'And when did Mr Josh Langley assure you of my abilities?'

'Today. He called from Europe to make sure everything was on schedule and to wish you luck. He said he tried the house first, but there was no answer, so he asked me to relay the message. Said he had an important engagement and wouldn't have time to try calling you again. Guess I forgot to mention it. A problem came up just before I left and we were running so late by the time

I got home.' There was an apology in his tone.

'That's okay.' She didn't want Mr Joshua Langley's wishes anyway. An uninvited image of the man holding Selena Smythe in his arms flashed into her mind, and her stomach began to churn while angry tears burned at the back of her eyes.

'You're suddenly very quiet,' Howard commented.

Swallowing the lump that had built in her throat, Jamie said, 'I just realised how very tired I am. These past few weeks have been rather strenuous.'

'I know.' He patted her hand. 'I've already said it several times this evening, but I have to say it again—I'm so very proud of the way you've handled yourself.'

'That means a great deal to me.' Uncontrolled tears escaped from her eyes.

'I didn't mean to make you cry.'

'I'm just so pleased that you're proud of me,' she said, glad to have a positive outlet for the tension that had built within her. 'Women commonly cry when they're happy. You wouldn't want to deny me a privilege I've worked so hard to earn.'

'No, I guess not,' he replied dubiously, his tone indicating that he would never understand the female mind.

In her bed later that night she promised herself she would put Josh Langley out of her life and mind for ever. However, the next morning, as in the past, she found that the promise was not so easily kept. Around ten o'clock a knock sounded on the door, and when she answered the summons she discovered a delivery boy with a gigantic box of red, pink, white and yellow long-stemmed roses. The wire inside the box was from Josh, congratulating her on her success of the night before. Two vases were required to hold all the flowers and her hands shook slightly as she arranged them.

'Ouch!' A cry of pain escaped as she pricked her finger on one of the yellow roses. Yellow. The colour reminded her of Selena. 'If I'd been a man he would have sent cigars,' she muttered, her perspective once again restored.

When her uncle arrived home that evening he commented on the flowers, only to be puzzled by her indifferent attitude. 'I thought you women always loved receiving these expensive little beauties,' he remarked.

'It's the sender who's important,' she replied.

'Speaking of the sender, Josh called again today. He'll be back in a few days.'

'It's too bad I won't be here,' Jamie responded coolly, no regret in her voice. 'You can thank him for the flowers for me.'

'I can't do that,' Howard shook his head. 'He specifically requested that you be here. He feels it's time to discuss the contest he mentioned. We're well into August and he wants to arrange this competition before the end of the summer.'

'Terrific,' Jamie muttered under her breath. 'And for Christmas he probably has plans for a little Jamie Kynter doll. You wind it up and it obeys your every command.'

'If you feel that way maybe you should go off for a while,' Howard suggested in a concerned tone. 'I'll tell Josh you were gone when I got home.'

'No, I won't have you lying for me.' There was resolve in her tone. 'I've seen this business through this far. I might as well stay for the rest of the show. I have to—I *am* the show.'

Howard gave his niece a comforting hug. 'You're just tired,' he diagnosed. 'Why don't you go to bed early? I'm sure things will look much brighter to you tomorrow.'

Jamie was not so certain. She recalled Josh's parting, the way he had treated her like a child, like his ward. He had even used the word nursemaid.

And then there was Selena. The blonde had made her intention of getting the man back crystal clear, and she'd had more than two weeks in Europe to accomplish this feat.

'I don't want Josh Langley taking care of me,' she muttered aloud in the privacy of her shower. 'Let Selena have him!'

Angry tears surfaced to add a saltiness to the clear water cascading over her face.

CHAPTER SEVEN

It was two days later, around eight-thirty in the morning, as Jamie was preparing to sit down at her desk to work, that she saw a strange car coming down her driveway. The compact blue coupé came to a halt in front of the house and as she watched through the front window, a woman in what looked to be her mid-fifties climbed laboriously out and limped towards the door using a cane for support. Her ankle, although not in a cast, was securely wrapped in an elastic bandage and the shoe which would normally have encased the foot had been replaced by a house slipper.

Opening the door, just as the woman rang the bell, Jamie startled her caller. 'I'm sorry,' she apologised, catching the woman's arm to steady her.

'That's all right, miss. I'm not normally so unsteady on my feet, but I sprained my ankle early this morning and it seems to be getting worse by the minute.'

'You should go home and sit with an ice pack on it,' Jamie advised.

'That's precisely what I'm hoping to do and why I'm here on your doorstep at this moment. This is Howard Kynter's doorstep, isn't it?'

'Yes.'

'And you're the girl in the pictures!' A pleased smile spread across the woman's face. 'I didn't realise it at first. I'm afraid this foot is bothering me more than I imagined.'

'I'm Jamie Kynter,' Jamie confirmed, then feeling uncomfortable about making the woman stand on the painful joint, she added, 'Would you like to come in and sit down?'

'Thank you, dear, I would. But only for a minute. There's so much to do.' Hobbling into the living room, the small, slightly plump female lowered herself into a chair. 'I never knew an ankle could throb so!'

Jamie took the chair opposite her. 'You know who I am, but I still have no idea who you are.'

'How rude of me! It's the pain. I'm not thinking too clearly, and that's why I have come to see your father.'

'My father is dead.' Jamie felt suddenly very ill at ease. When she had invited the woman in, it had been under the assumption that this person knew her uncle, but this was obviously not the case.

'I'm sorry, dear—I simply assumed you were Howard Kynter's daughter since the name is the same. Don't tell me you're his wife.'

For some reason this idea seemed to upset the grey-haired woman greatly and Jamie felt compelled to dispel this false notion. 'I'm his niece.'

'Oh!' the caller breathed a sigh of relief. Then as if feeling the need to add something said, 'That's nice.'

Jamie decided that she had had as much of this incoherent conversation as she could handle. 'Would you, please, tell me your name and exactly why you're here?' she requested firmly.

'I'm Maggie—Maggie Newby.' The woman pronounced her name as if it should mean something to Jamie and extended her hand in greeting.

'I'm pleased to meet you, Miss Newby,' Jamie responded dubiously, accepting the handshake.

'It's Mrs Newby. I'm a widow. And I really do need to see your uncle.'

'He isn't here,' Jamie's voice held a note of apology.

'Oh, dear! When will he be back? Or can I reach him at work? I really do need his help. It's this darn ankle, and there's so much to do.'

'My uncle is out of town until tomorrow. Perhaps if you tell me what you want I can be of some assistance,' Jamie encouraged.

'Would you? That would be wonderful!' The woman's face brightened considerably.

'If you would simply tell me why you're here.'

'Joshua said I should call on Howard Kynter if I needed any help.'

'Joshua? Joshua Langley?' There was a sharp edge to Jamie's voice.

'Yes, I'm his housekeeper. Surely your uncle mentioned me?'

'Anything not imminently connected with the magazine readily slips Uncle Howard's mind.' Jamie suddenly felt apprehensive. 'Has anything . . . anything happened to Josh?'

'Oh, no, nothing like that. It's the movers. They're bringing in the furniture today, although there's already a lot of furniture at the house. Joshua bought several pieces from Mr and Mrs Steward when he purchased their place, but then we're moving from an apartment and there was room for plenty more to fill that old house.'

'I see.' A hard lump formed in Jamie's throat. So Josh had purchased the Stewards' house! If he and Selena remarried she would not be able to avoid running into them periodically. This thought disturbed her, forcing her to admit that she had been rash in assuring him that his proximity would not affect her.

'You look as pale as I feel,' Maggie remarked, drawing her attention back to the present situation.

'I'm fine,' she assured the woman, while inwardly wishing that all this was just a nightmare and she would wake up soon. 'What can I do to help you?'

'I'm afraid I have to ask a great deal. I was wondering if you'd mind very much coming over to the house and helping me unload the groceries I have in the car. Then when the movers arrive I could use some help in making certain they put everything in the right place.'

The last thing in the world Jamie wanted was to involve herself in Joshua Langley's home, but it was obvious Maggie Newby was in a great deal of pain, and there was no one else she could turn to. Jamie forced a smile. 'Of course I don't mind. Just let me get some ice for your ankle in case no one filled the ice trays over at the Stewards.'

'I appreciate this.' A grimace of pain appeared on Maggie's face as she moved her foot. 'Joshua assured me that he'd hired a cleaning service to scrub out the place and unpack the new appliances and set them into order. But you never can be sure if the people got the job done.'

'Josh Langley usually gets what he wants done.' The touch of cynicism in Jamie's tone went unnoticed by Maggie, who nodded in a pleased manner.

'Yes, Joshua's a real powerhouse when he sets his mind to something.' There was pride in the older woman's voice, making it apparent that she adored her employer.

'I'll follow you over in my car,' Jamie directed, returning to the living room a few minutes later with the ice in a plastic bag.

'Fine,' Maggie agreed, but when she tried to rise her pallor became a dusty grey.

'Have you seen a doctor?'

'I didn't have time.' The response was coupled with a low moan as the woman sank back into the chair. 'I was on my way out of the door this morning when this happened and I had a long drive ahead of me. I honestly didn't think it was all that bad at the time. I hobbled down to the local drugstore and bought this bandage and cane. The drive down wasn't all that difficult either. It really only started throbbing when I was walking around in the grocery store.'

'I'm taking you to see Dr Evans before we go to the Steward house.' Jamie's tone indicated that she would not accept a refusal. 'And since you're in no condition to drive, I'll drive your car.' Taking the woman's arm, she directed Maggie to lean on her as she helped the older woman out to the vehicle.

'I do hope we won't be too long at the doctor's,' Maggie fussed. 'The movers are due this morning.'

Jamie made no response, remembering all the times she had sat for hours waiting to be treated. As she feared, the doctor's office was full when they arrived.

'It will be a while before the doctor can see you,' the nurse apologised. 'I'll put you ahead on the list, but I'm sure Dr Evans will want to have X-rays taken.'

Settling Maggie into a chair, Jamie rewrapped the foot in the bags of ice and picked up a magazine to thumb through.

Maggie fidgeted. 'I can't stay here,' she blurted out after only a few minutes, making an attempt to stand. 'I've got to be at the house when the movers arrive and the ice cream is sure to have melted by now.'

'Please, calm down.' Jamie reseated the woman. 'You can't go running around on that ankle—it will only make it worse.'

'I'll stay if you'll go to the house and unpack the groceries that belong in the refrigerator and put a note on the door for the movers,' Maggie bargained.

'I don't know how you and Josh get along living in the same house. You're as insistent on having your own way as he is!' Jamie returned, with a shake of her head.

Maggie rewarded this observation with a conspiratorial wink. 'I'll tell you a secret. Joshua's putty in your hands if you know how to handle him.'

'It's impossible for me to imagine Josh Langley being putty in anyone's hands,' Jamie noted sceptically.

'Maybe not exactly putty,' Maggie amended. 'But he is very warm and generous and would change the world for someone he loved.'

Or just for his own enjoyment, Jamie thought caustically. Not wanting to get into a discussion concerning her views of Josh, she rose. 'I'd better get going.'

'I really do appreciate this.' Fumbling in her purse, Maggie produced the key. As she handed the small silverish object to Jamie, she had a second thought.

'There's no sense in you coming back here until I'm finished. Why don't you wait at the house and call here every once in a while? Joshua said he'd had the phones installed. He didn't want me being out there with no way to communicate with the outside world in case of trouble. That man is so considerate—but then I'm sure you know that.'

Again Jamie forced a smile.

'Then when I'm finished you can come and get me. There's no sense in both of us sitting around this office all morning. Meanwhile, if the movers show up you can direct them. All the boxes are clearly labeled. Joshua's things go in the master bedroom. You do know the house?'

'I'm familiar with the layout.' Arranging Josh's bedroom had never crossed Jamie's mind when she had agreed to help. A strong protest rose from deep within her, but the grey pallor of the woman's face stopped its issuance. Attempting to ignore the knot in her stomach, she returned her attention to the directions Maggie was giving in a quick precise flow.

'And the books in the library. Now I've never been in the house, but Joshua says there's a suite of rooms downstairs off the kitchen.'

'Yes, where Mrs Steward's mother lived before her death. There's a bedroom, a sitting room and a bathroom.'

'That's where my things will go.' Maggie dropped her head into her hands. 'I can't believe I'm here with this awful ankle, and there's so much to do.'

'Please, don't worry. I'll take care of everything,' Jamie assured her, while wishing she could go home and lock herself in her room instead.

'Thank you, dear.' Maggie rewarded her with a smile. 'The minute I saw your pictures, I knew you'd be sweet and considerate.'

Jamie shook her head at the perplexity of human nature. Why would a person spend as much time examining the pictures of her in *Meadow and Brook* as the housekeeper's conversation implied and not have taken the time to read the article or, at the very least, scanned it? But apparently Maggie had done just that because she hadn't known that Howard Kynter was not Jamie's father.

The house Josh had purchased, like the one which Jamie and her uncle shared, was built of native stone, the original section having been constructed in the late 1900s. A great deal of renovating had been done to the interior to bring it up to modern standards plus several rooms had been added. Even so, the place retained an atmosphere of history. The Stewards had furnished their home with antiques of the Colonial period, giving it an atmosphere of genteel comfort. Many times, Jamie had sat in front of the huge stone hearth in the kitchen, decorated with iron pots and brass bed warmers, and pictured Colonial women cooking over the fire while children in long dresses and breeches played on the floor nearby.

But today when she entered, the atmosphere was different; less calm, less peaceful. Josh had bought some of the Stewards' best pieces and even the iron pots and bed warmers still stood around the stone hearth. But today she thought of soldiers and wars, muskets and cannons.

Although the original hearth had been preserved along with a semi-circular portion of the stone floor, the back wall of the kitchen had been knocked out and the room enlarged to hold numerous cabinets and all the modern appliances. As Josh had promised his house-keeper, the house was clean and the appliances had been unpacked, hooked up, wiped out, and ready for use.

Moving quickly, as if trying to outrun her thoughts and disturbing emotions, she carried in the groceries. Unpacking the articles which needed refrigeration, she left the rest neatly arranged on the counter, knowing that Maggie would want to organise her kitchen for herself.

Calling the doctor's office, she was informed that Mrs Newby was at the lab having X-rays taken. Jamie paced nervously around the house. She couldn't shake off the feeling of Josh's presence. The man seemed to be invading every nook and cranny of her world.

'The problem with Josh Langley is . . . ,' she began aloud in an effort to put words to her jumbled feelings about this man whom she had met so dramatically in the middle of a storm and who had caused her to feel as if she was living in the eye of a hurricane ever since, waiting for the end of the storm to hit and then pass leaving devastation in its path. '. . . it's me,' she completed the statement. Why did she continuously overreact to the man?

She was so engrossed in her thoughts that a loud pounding on the front door caused her to jump nervously. It was the movers, and she found herself unhappily caught in the turmoil of directing traffic. The boxes were clearly marked as Maggie had promised, but arranging Josh's house with Selena in the back of her mind as its new mistress was not a job she relished.

When she was finally able to escape for a moment and call the doctor's office again it was to be told that Mrs Newby was now in with the doctor.

'This here bed is marked for the master bedroom, lady,' one of the men said in a questioning tone as she rejoined the activity.

'Upstairs. First door on the left,' she instructed, watching the men carry the heavy brass headboard past her. 'Josh and Selena's bed,' a voice taunted her. 'Who cares?' she retorted. 'You care,' came the response.

'Lady,' an impatient male voice demanded from directly behind her, 'this settee is labelled for a Mrs Newby?'

'It goes in the first room off the kitchen.' Pulling her mind away from its destructive path, she followed the man to be certain he put the piece of furniture in the sitting room and not in the bedroom.

The ringing of the phone startled her. Then remembering that she had left the phone number with the nurse after her last futile attempt to reach Maggie, she picked it up with a sense of relief.

'I'm finished at last!' Maggie announced triumphantly over the instrument.

Seeking out the man in charge of the movers, Jamie explained that she had to leave for a few minutes in order to pick up Mrs Newby. Glancing at his watch he decided that it was a good time for his men to stop for lunch, thus she left them sitting under an elm tree in the front yard exchanging stories and eating as she drove off.

When she arrived at the doctor's office, the nurse directed her to wait a moment, explaining that the doctor wanted to have a few words with her. Maggie began to protest, but Jamie, who felt the need to sit down away from Josh's unnerving presence if only for a few minutes, assured her that the movers were perfectly happy and would be there whenever they returned.

'I'm usually easier to get along with. More likeable,' the older woman said, reseating herself. 'But today has been so very frustrating.'

Any day involving Josh Langley can be frustrating, Jamie mused to herself, while aloud she said, 'I like you just fine,' and to her surprise, realised that she meant it. Mrs Newby had caused her a great deal of trouble. Still, the woman possessed an amiable quality.

'I must say that I like you. I'm so pleased Joshua found you.'

Jamie was about to make a sharp remark she might later regret when the doctor appeared. 'Jamie, Mrs Newby tells me you're helping her with this moving business.'

'Yes, Dr Evans,' she confirmed.

'Good. I want you to be certain she follows my instructions to the letter. She's to remain off that foot as much as possible for the next few days. It must be elevated and packed in ice for the rest of today and tonight. Nothing is broken, and if she follows my instructions, within a few days she should be able to get around pretty well.'

'I'll see she follows your instructions,' Jamie promised, while Maggie frowned.

'I'm not a baby and I don't need a nursemaid! This young lady has been gracious enough to help me with the movers, but I refuse to ask her to babysit me.'

'You're not asking her.' The doctor's tone was firm. 'I'm telling her,' the finality in his voice putting an end to any further protests.

Maggie shook her head in exasperation. 'I knew I should have come down here yesterday,' she said as Jamie guided the car out of the parking lot. 'But Joshua was so insistent that I stay and enjoy my grandchildren until the last minute. They're such darlings.' Here she paused to sigh pleasantly at the thought of the children, then hurried on, asking, 'How's the moving going?'

'They've unloaded the furniture and most of the boxes. I would say they're about ready to begin unpacking.'

'I want to wash the dishes before they're put away,' Maggie said half to herself and half aloud, as her mind busily organised the afternoon's activities. 'They can start in the library—there are tons of books to unpack. I want to unpack the linens myself, but they can take the clothes out of the hanging boxes and put them into the closets.' To Jamie's relief Maggie continued in this business vein during the entire drive home, not once turning the conversation towards their mutual employer.

Back at the house, she allowed Maggie into the kitchen only long enough to outline how she wanted the room arranged. Then propelling the housekeeper into the library, Jamie sat her down on the couch and, propping her foot up, rewrapped the ankle in a fresh bag of ice.

'I'll bring you some lunch and you can sit here and direct the men while they unload the books and files. I'll eat in the kitchen and run the dishes through the dishwasher.'

'I didn't mean for you to work all day,' Maggie protested.

'I really don't mind,' Jamie assured her. She didn't feel she could leave the woman alone after promising the doctor she would look after her, and keeping busy was the only way she could keep her mind off of the new owner.

In the kitchen she unpacked dishes, washed pots and pans, lined shelves and put things away. After which she moved into Maggie's rooms and unpacked towels and linens, made the bed, and in general made the room livable in. Returning to the kitchen to unload another batch of dishes from the dishwasher, she discovered Maggie hobbling towards her.

'I've sent the men away. They've done all they can do. The rest is up to me.'

'There you're wrong,' Jamie responded firmly. 'You may go into your room and lie down or go into the living room and prop your foot up, but you're not going to do any unpacking today. I promised the doctor, remember.'

'But Joshua's bedroom has to be arranged. He'll be home tomorrow or the next day at the latest and I did so want to have everything ready. I was even planning to fry chicken tonight so he could have it for lunch tomorrow if he was early. That man loves cold fried chicken.'

'I'll unpack the boxes in the master bedroom,' Jamie said, her back muscles tightening with displeasure. 'And I'll fry the chicken, but you have to stay off of that ankle.'

'You can skip the chicken. However, I will accept your offer to unpack Joshua's things,' Maggie conceded, with a small pout.

Steeling herself, Jamie climbed the stairs as if she expected a goblin to pop out in front of her at any moment. 'A goblin of your own making,' she chided herself. In the hallway she stopped to unload a box of linen belonging in the oversized closet outside the guest bathroom. But she could not postpone the inevitable for ever and the time came when she was forced to go into the master bedroom. This room had been part of the original house and contained its own fireplace, adding a cosiness to the atmosphere. She could picture the fire burning lazily as soft snow fell on the trees outside and the two occupants of the bed snuggled together. 'No!' the word exploded angrily from her mouth.

Forcing the scene out of her mind, she opened and emptied boxes with precision and speed. In less than two hours the bed was made, the adjoining bathroom stocked, and all the boxes except for one unpacked. Opening this final container, she found a folded gold frame among the contents. It was the size for holding two eight by ten-inch photographs and had been carefully wrapped to prevent breakage. Assuming that she would find Selena and Josh smiling at one another on the inside, she started to lay the unopened frame on the dresser. A masochistic urge changed her mind. Opening the frame, she hoped that this last assault would put Josh Langley out of her thoughts for ever.

Sinking on to the corner of the bed in shock, she stared down at the photographs. She had been mistaken. They weren't of Josh and Selena but of her. One showed her sitting on the rock in the middle of the stream behind her home and the other was of her in her straw hat making a playful face at the photographer.

As the surprise wore off, she recognised them as being two of the pictures Joe Marley had taken for the magazine cover. Or more accurately, one had been taken for the cover and the other had been taken when she was kidding around during a break.

It was these photographs Maggie had been referring to. This realisation struck Jamie like a light bulb coming on in a dark room, clarifying several remarks the woman had made. Obviously, the housekeeper was under the impression that Jamie was Josh's newest love interest. However, Jamie knew that wasn't the reason for the photographs adorning his room. He had them framed and displayed in the same spirit a trainer displays pictures of his prize animals. Closing the frame with a snap, she placed it on the dresser, her mouth set in a hard straight line. Finishing quickly, she left, closing the door behind her as if she could lock her thoughts of Josh in the room and free herself of his haunting presence.

Back downstairs she found Maggie on her knees unpacking a box of figurines. 'And just what do you think you're doing?' she demanded, her voice sounding angrier than she meant it to because of strain and exhaustion.

'Now, don't you be mad at me! I simply couldn't stand to see that box just sitting there.'

'What am I going to do with you?' A relenting smile curved Jamie's lips.

'You can have dinner and spend the night,' Maggie suggested promptly. 'I have to confess that I feel a bit nervous, with this being my first night in this big old house and my not being able to move around very well.'

Although Jamie was not enthusiastic about sleeping under Josh's roof, she felt compelled to agree. Maggie was still in a great deal of pain and she couldn't bring herself to desert the older woman after such a strenuous day. Besides, she was certain that the minute she was out of the door, Maggie would be back unpacking boxes. 'I'll stay and then tomorrow morning we'll finish the unpacking together. You can direct from the couch and I'll do all the leg work. Agreed?'

'Agreed!' Maggie smiled.

During dinner, the housekeeper talked incessantly about her family, a topic for which Jamie was deeply grateful because it kept her mind off Josh. However, towards the end of the meal, Maggie did steer the conversation around to her employer. 'I've worked for

Joshua for eleven years now. He's almost like my own son. We've been through a lot together—mostly good, though I have to admit I've seen him through some rough times, too. That marriage of his . . .' Here she paused to shake her head.

Having no desire to hear about how painful his divorce had been, Jamie quickly pushed her chair away from the table before Maggie could continue. 'I'm beat. Why don't I help you into bed and we can both get a good night's sleep?'

Yawning widely, Maggie nodded in agreement.

After tucking the woman in for the night, Jamie placed a small silver bell on the night stand next to the bed. 'I'll be on the couch in your sitting room. If you need me, just ring the bell.'

'You can't sleep on that couch—your muscles will cramp. I won't allow it, not with all the guest rooms upstairs.'

'I can't hear the bell if I'm upstairs,' Jamie noted patiently.

'Well, what's that box on the wall, right over my head?' Maggie frowned, then before Jamie could respond, answered the question herself. 'It's an intercom, isn't it?'

'Yes. It runs throughout the lower level of the house, but the only bedroom it's hooked up to is the master bedroom. Mrs Steward's mother was ill and they used it to check on her and she used it to call them if she needed assistance.'

'How does it work?'

'You throw this switch to turn it on and press this button to be heard. Then you have to release the button for the person on the other end to talk to you.' Jamie demonstrated.

'That seems kind of complicated for an in-house intercom.'

'It is.' Jamie smiled playfully. 'They had a simpler one, but discovered that Mrs Wiley was listening to them constantly. This one allows the people on either end to be contacted while retaining their privacy.'

'You must sleep in Joshua's room. That's the only solution,' Maggie insisted. 'That way you'll have a comfortable bed in which to rest and I'll be able to reach you easily if that becomes necessary.'

'The couch will be perfectly comfortable,' Jamie returned firmly.

'I know Joshua won't mind, and I can't stand the idea of you sleeping on the couch. I feel guilty enough about all the trouble I've caused.' Maggie's mouth formed a hard determined line.

Exhausted, and worried that if she argued with the woman further she might reveal more than she wanted to regarding her feelings towards Josh Langley, Jamie capitulated. After a warm shower, she climbed hesitantly in between the soft cotton sheets of the man's bed. Her clothes lay on a chair nearby. Having no nightgown to wear, she had taken one of his robes out of the closet and thrown it on the foot of the bed in case she needed to check on Maggie during the night. Switching on the intercom, she pressed the button. 'Goodnight, Maggie,' she said into the mouthpiece, feeling anything but good.

'Goodnight, Jamie,' came the response, interrupted by a yawn. 'Sleep tight.'

Sleep. That was the one thing Jamie was certain she would not be able to accomplish lying in this huge bed surrounded by Josh's presence. However, the hard physical exercise of the day came to her aid and almost as soon as she lay back on the pillow, her eyes closed and she was lost in the realm of dreams.

A soft smile played on her lips as a hand gently stroked her arm before moving sensually down the length of her sheet covered body and then back again to touch her cheek. Feather-light kisses fell on her face and shoulders. A deep longing sigh issued from her throat.

The dream was so real. Even as she left the depths of

sleep, the touch, the sensation of the lips, even the masculine smell lingered, filling her senses and awakening long-hidden desires.

The warm caressing hands removed the barrier of the sheet and circled beneath her to test the smoothness of her back while the teasing lips found her mouth. Her palms rested against her seducer's shirt, luxuriating in the feel of his hot hard muscles beneath the fabric. It all seemed so real.

Abandoning their provocative play on her mouth, the warm mobile lips sought out her ear lobe and nibbled gently. 'You're not only beautiful but you taste delicious,' a male voice breathed in a harsh whisper.

Her hands moved upward to circle her dream lover's neck as she arched her body closer to his.

'Jamie.' Her name was pronounced in a low sensual moan. 'You had me fooled, you know. I bought that innocent girl-next-door image.'

Something was wrong. The man felt too real. He sounded too real. Her eyes popped open. He *was* real.

'Josh!' The name came out in a startled gasp as her arms slid limply from his neck while her sleep-clogged mind tried to decipher where the dream had ended and reality begun.

'I apologise for waking you,' he murmured with a quiet laugh. There was no remorse in his voice as his lips played in the hollow of her neck. 'I would have waited until morning, but you looked so very appetising I couldn't resist a taste.' To emphasise his words, he nibbled on her shoulder causing goosebumps to rise on her sensitive skin.

She tried to think, but her mind wouldn't work. His touch commanded her senses, her very being, sparking newer more potent fires with every heartbeat.

'Won't your uncle worry about where you are, or does he think you're off on one of your fishing expeditions?' Josh was looking down on to her passion-flushed features, a slightly amused gleam in his dark eyes.

'He's out of town until tomorrow.' Her voice sounded regretful, as if the time was too short.

His hand moved along her ribcage to cup her breast. 'Then it's a good thing I came back a day early,' he murmured as his mouth followed the line of her throat down to taste the rosy peak at his fingertips.

'Yes,' she moaned with pleasure, then as a picture of Selena impinged on her mind a harsh 'No!' followed.

Undaunted, his hands continued their erotic exploration of her desire-awakened body. 'No,' he mocked her, tasting the sweetness of her other breast before returning to claim her mouth once more.

Twisting her head to free her lips, Jamie hissed, 'You were with Selena!' She struggled against him now, but his strength was much greater than hers.

'So you're the jealous type,' he returned in a throaty, pleased laugh, not denying the accusation. Stretching out on the bed, he pinned her body beneath him. 'Jamie, stop struggling,' he commanded.

She felt his need and, despite Selena, trembled with the desire to fulfil that need.

'Jamie!' Her name was being called, but it wasn't Josh's voice. 'Jamie, are you all right?'

He pulled away from her in shocked surprise.

'Jamie, answer me!' the voice demanded.

'Who? What?' Josh questioned sharply.

'Maggie . . . intercom,' she answered incoherently, feeling disorientated by her sudden freedom.

'Maggie?' Swinging his legs off the bed and himself into a sitting position, he ran a hand through his hair.

The housekeeper's voice sounded again over the instrument and he turned to Jamie. 'How do you work the damn thing? I don't want her coming up here.'

'Press the button to talk. Release it to hear,' she managed to choke out as she pulled the sheet up around her to hide her nakedness, while tears of anger at herself and this man who so easily overcame her defences filled her eyes.

'Jamie's all right, Maggie,' he said into the mouth-piece. 'I gave her a bit of a scare, but I'm sure she'll survive.'

'Joshua, is that you?' came the startled response.

'Yes—now go back to sleep.'

'Wait a minute!' Jamie found her voice. Tucking the sheet more securely around herself, she raised up to a level where she could speak into the intercom and pressing the button asked in a voice that shocked her by its steadiness, 'Maggie, do you need anything?'

'No. I guess Joshua must have woken me when he came in. Anyway, I was awake and couldn't get back to sleep and I thought I heard noises. Of course, in an old house like this I know it's natural to hear noises, but I finally decided to call and make sure you were okay.'

'Goodnight, then.' Jamie released the button and sank back on to the pillow, her arms weak and her body shaken.

'I didn't see her car when I drove in. Why didn't you tell me she was downstairs?' Josh questioned as he finished unbuttoning his shirt and discarded it on to the chair which housed her clothes.

'Her car is behind the garage and she can't barge anywhere. Her ankle is swollen,' Jamie explained weak-ly, the sight of his dark curly-haired chest looming above her, frightening and exciting her both at the same time.

'And what kind of yarn did you spin to get her to let you stay in my bedroom?' There was a slightly cruel twist to his mouth as he captured the sheet and attempted to bare her once more.

'I didn't spin any yarn, as you put it.' She clutched the sheet securely. 'She came to the house this morning and asked for help, so I helped. You weren't supposed to be home until tomorrow and this is the only bedroom with an intercom. She wouldn't let me sleep on the couch.' Tears were flowing freely now as she fought the shame her behaviour had evoked. Adding to her despair was the realisation that even in her shame, she wanted him.

A shuttered look came into his eyes as her explanation poured out. When she finished he sat silently, avoiding looking at her, his jaw set in a grim line. 'You don't have to hold the sheet so tightly,' he said at last. 'I'm not going to attack you.' Rising from the bed, he picked up his shirt. 'And don't feel so badly. I'll take all the blame for this mistake.'

Jamie lay rigid until the door closed behind him, then burying her face in the pillow to muffle the sound, cried until she had no more tears. She could no longer deny her love for this man who saw her only as an object of his lust and disdained her when she could not freely give herself to him to fulfil his animal needs. As the tears subsided, she considered leaving. But how would she explain her flight to Maggie? And then there was Josh. She could imagine his contemptuous laugh when he discovered she had fled like a child in the night.

She lay awake until nearly dawn, her eyes sore and swollen, her heart bruised and bleeding. Then, crawling out of the bed like a wounded animal, she wrote a note containing Dr Evans' name and address and his instructions concerning Maggie's ankle. Let Josh think what he would; she could not remain under his roof any longer.

Dropping the note on the kitchen table, she left through the back door. The dew was heavy on the grass, shimmering silvery in the pre-dawn light, while a lone bird sang its solitary song.

'Leaving without saying goodbye?'

She spun around to discover Josh sitting on the patio. He was still dressed in the clothes he had been wearing in the bedroom, and she wondered if he had been out there all this time. 'I left a note about Maggie's ankle . . . the doctor's name and phone number and his instructions.' She spoke evenly, slowly, like a person in daze, too drained to show any emotion.

'Jamie, we have to talk.' There was a grimness about his expression and she knew he hadn't slept any more than she had since their encounter in the bedroom.

'When I found you in my bed, I didn't think. I wanted to believe you were there waiting for me, so I jumped to a hasty, inexcusable conclusion. You left a lot unfinished when you ran away from me that night of the storm.'

'How arrogant you are!' She turned on him hurtfully, hoping to wound him as deeply as he had wounded her. 'You think every woman is ready to fall panting into your arms. Well, I wouldn't want you if you were the last man on earth!'

'I know you don't mean that. You're just tired—we both are. I want you to get some rest and we'll talk later.'

'If you want someone to talk to, go and find Selena,' she threw over her shoulder as she moved purposefully away from him.

Josh rose, falling into step beside her. 'I wasn't with Selena. I don't know where you got that idea, but it's not true.'

'You didn't deny it earlier. You practically admitted it.'

'I did not. I admitted being pleased that you were jealous and that was all.'

'I don't believe you!'

'Suit yourself, but let me drive you home. This grass is wet and it's a good mile and a half to your house.'

'No, thanks. I'll walk—I need the fresh air.' Jamie continued across the lawn towards the trees, expecting him to stop, but he stayed with her. Wishing to avoid any physical contact, she maintained a distance of a foot or more between them at all times. As if he sensed her need not to be touched, Josh hooked his hands loosely into his pants pockets and kept his distance.

It was not until she had unlocked the back door of her house and was preparing to go in that he laid a restraining hand on her arm and broke the silence between them. 'Who did you think I was?' The question was not asked in a mocking tone. There was a sense of urgency in his voice, a need to know.

'I was dreaming. People in dreams don't have faces,'

she hedged as she attempted to pull away from his grasp.

'Who was the man in your dream, Jamie?' His dark eyes probed her face.

'It was you. Are you satisfied!' she admitted through clenched teeth.

He released her then and she flew inside, locking the door securely behind her. Her head throbbed. She wished she had lied and wondered why she had told him the truth. Too exhausted to think, she kicked off her wet shoes and throwing herself down on the couch in the living room, fell into a restless sleep. When she awoke her neck felt stiff, but her mind was less groggy. Making herself a cup of coffee, she tried to think more clearly about what had transpired between herself and Josh Langley.

Maybe she was wrong about the man. This insiduous thought, more hope than reason, taunted her as she drank her coffee on the patio staring across the lawn they had traversed together before dawn. She recalled the look on his face when she had admitted the identity of the man in her dreams. It hadn't been triumphant or mocking. It had been a look of relief.

Maybe he hadn't forced himself on her because he really cared about her and not because he wasn't interested enough. And he had denied being with Selena.

Her uncle liked him and Maggie adored him. They couldn't both be totally wrong. Thinking back over her association with him, Jamie had to admit that she had never really given herself a chance to know the man. He had said they would talk and she made up her mind to listen.

He called around noon. 'I'm going to have to stay with Maggie today to see that she follows the doctor's orders, and I have an appointment this evening I can't avoid,' he explained apologetically. 'But I'm clearing my calendar for tomorrow, so you and I will have the entire day to ourselves. I'll be at your place by nine in the morning.'

Jamie's hands were shaking when she hung up. She

felt like a teenager who had just been asked out on her first date. In a state of nervous excitement, she went up to her room and scanned her closet, trying to decide what to wear. Her contemplations were suddenly interrupted by a loud knocking on the front door. The caller was impatient, banging the brass knocker several more times before she could answer the summons. In her heart, she wanted it to be Josh. She wanted him to tell her that he couldn't wait until tomorrow to talk to her, to be with her.

But when she opened the door, the smile on her face froze at the sight of Selena Smythe standing on her doorstep.

'I was on my way to see Josh's new house and I simply had to stop by to tell you how excited Barbara was about your show. She seems to feel that the sportswear line will be a smashing success, and from the photos I've seen, I must say that I agree.' As she spoke, Selena moved past Jamie and into the living room, where she seated herself in one of the wingbacked chairs near the fireplace.

'Thank you,' Jamie responded dubiously, not believing for one minute that this was the woman's real reason for coming by to see her.

'It was a shame Josh wasn't able to attend.'

'He was busy.'

'Yes, I know.' The shrewd smile on the blonde's face shook Jamie's fragile world. 'You realise, I'm sure, that it had to be something or someone very important to him to keep him away.'

'Yes, I realise that.' A coldness filled Jamie. He had lied to her. What she didn't understand was why Selena felt compelled to flaunt their relationship.

'Of course, once he starts a project he hates to leave it until it's what he terms a total success. I feel certain he hasn't deserted you yet.' The woman's tone made a question out of this last statement, causing Jamie to realise that Selena was not as confident about her recapture of Josh as she wished to appear.

'No, not totally,' she admitted, getting very little satisfaction out of the blonde's discomfort.

'I only hope for your sake that you're able to walk away from this association with Josh unscathed.' Selena's voice took on a sage-like quality. 'He can have a very devastating effect on a woman's life. Believe me, I know.'

Jamie felt as if she was being patted on the head and told to play with children her own age and leave the adults alone. A seething anger burned within her and she hoped Selena would leave before she said something they might both regret.

As if sensing her mission was complete, Selena rose and moved towards the door. 'For your sake, I hope you'll keep in mind that playing with Josh is like playing with fire.' In the entrance hall she paused to run her hand over the thick plaster wall. 'I'm so pleased he bought one of these older houses, they're so sturdy. But then he knows I catch cold with the slightest draft.'

The implication of this last remark was not lost on Jamie. Selena was letting her know that by winter she expected to be living under Josh's roof. Following her unwelcome guest's departure, Jamie stood for a long time hugging herself tightly to stop the shaking. 'I suppose I should be grateful to her for warning me,' she muttered, as bitter tears burned at the back of her eyes.

Regaining control, she climbed the stairs and began packing. She knew exactly what she was doing. She was running away from the man again. Maybe it was childish, but for her it was an act of survival.

'I can't wait around all summer for Josh Langley to decide what he wants to do next with my life,' she told her uncle when he arrived home that evening to find her car packed and Jamie perusing maps and drawing up an extensive itinerary.

'He's already decided.' Howard handed her a manila envelope. 'That's the outline for the contest. He sent it over by messenger today for Grace to type up with the

instructions that he would pick it up and go over the
details with you himself some time later this week. I
thought since she finished it today you should have an
opportunity to look it over and be ready with suggestions
or changes you might want to make when he does talk to
you.'

Jamie swallowed back the tears of humiliation. She
had played the fool again. The talk Josh had been so
insistent on having with her tomorrow was nothing more
than a build-up to cajole her into going along with this
latest scheme. Selena needn't have been worried after
all. 'I'll look it over tonight and write out any suggestions
or alternations I think would be appropriate,' she said
tightly, 'and you can deliver them to Mr Langley yourself, because by seven tomorrow morning I'll be on my
way to Ohio and points west.'

Howard took a long narrow look at his niece. There
was no question in his mind that she meant what she said
and that no amount of pleading or reasoning would
change her mind.

That night she read over the proposal. The contest
would be unofficial, with each magazine covering it in its
own way. There would be no prior public announcement
made. The participants would meet merely as friends
entering into a private wager. Just to make it interesting,
Meadow and Brook was willing to put up five thousand
dollars to go to the winner.

Josh named Bennett Spring State Park as the site of
the competition, explaining that he had chosen a state
park used by the average fisherman because all the
contestants presumably wrote for and advised this seg-
ment of the population, therefore they should compete
under the same conditions in which the people they
advised had to fish. However, because they were experts, there were certain stipulations. First, they would
not start fishing until two hours after the beginning bell
had sounded. Secondly, to add variety to the competition, each of the contestants would have to catch at least

one of his five fish from each of the three specified lure zones into which the park stream was divided. Using unbarbed hooks, the participants could pick and choose which fish they wished to keep. At the end of the day, there would be a weigh-in and the person with the highest poundage would be declared the winner. This was to be strictly a one day only, rain or shine, competition, and he named October the tenth as the day.

Jamie found it difficult to concentrate. After struggling, through the proposal twice, fighting Josh's image in each word, she decided that it was complete and needed no suggestions from her. Shoving the papers back into the envelope, she added a quickly scribbled note. It began without a salutation and read: 'If your future plans for me hinge on the outcome of this competition then you should understand that considering the people involved, the winner will be determined by the luck of the draw and not by any special skill. It is my opinion that you should reconsider this scheme.' She signed it 'Duckbill's Daughter'.

When she returned the proposal to her uncle the next morning along with her message for Josh, she also handed him her itinerary, agreeing to call once a week and promising to be at Bennett Spring on October the tenth unless she heard otherwise from him.

'You don't like the idea of this competition very much, do you?' he questioned.

'No, not much. It isn't something my father would have agreed to.'

'I think you should talk to Josh about it, then. Tell him how you feel.'

'What I feel has never affected Mr Langley before and I'm sure it won't influence him this time.'

'I still think you should try.'

'I don't intend to have anything to do with Mr Josh Langley again unless it's absolutely necessary. You tell him how I feel—maybe he'll listen to you.'

'Jamie, I . . .'

'I don't want to argue with you just before I leave,' she interrupted. 'Let's drop this subject. I really do need to be on my way.'

Howard hugged his niece. 'I don't want to argue with you either. You go along now and have a good trip. I'll talk to Josh about this competition.'

Jamie left her uncle sitting on the patio indulging in a second cup of coffee. As she passed the phone in the hall she stopped. Licking her suddenly dry lips, she picked up the receiver and dialled Josh's number. To her relief, Maggie answered. 'Will you give our mutual employer a message for me,' she requested, keeping her voice businesslike. 'Tell him I won't be able to see him today. I've decided that there are several places I need to visit before the end of the summer and I must leave right away. Tell him, too, that I've read over the proposal for the contest. I don't like the idea of this competition, but if he insists, I'll be at Bennett Spring on October the tenth.'

'If you'll just wait one minute, I'll get Josh and you can give him your message personally,' Maggie encouraged. 'He's going to be very disappointed about not seeing you today.'

'I really can't wait. I have a schedule to keep,' Jamie lied. 'Please, give him my message.' She hung up before Maggie could make any further pleas or Josh could get to the phone.

As if she was suddenly worried that he would materialise out of thin air, she hurried out of the door and was on her way.

CHAPTER EIGHT

When she called her uncle later in the week as arranged, he told her that Josh wanted her at Bennett Spring on October tenth. 'I tried to talk him out of it. But he insisted,' Howard explained apologetically.

'He can be very insistent.'

'I'm going to keep trying,' he promised, but she knew it was a waste of time.

September wore slowly away. The contest itself wasn't what bothered her; she had already warned Josh about the possible outcome. What tormented her was his choice of the site. It was like a slap in the face. Attempting to be philosophical about the situation, Jamie told herself that the best way to bury the past was to meet it head on. When that didn't work, she argued that the park was a beautiful place and she should not let the fact that it was also where she had encountered Josh for the first time ruin this lovely piece of America for her.

Unable to bring herself to arrive at the park any sooner than was absolutely necessary, she had arranged her schedule so that she would arrive on October the ninth. As she turned off the Interstate on to State Route Sixty-four, the quiet Ozark countryside stretched out before her. Cattle wandered leisurely among the scrub pines, grazing on land too rocky to plough or resting in the shade of spreading oaks or maples. Wild daisies, their white petals swaying in the breeze, shared the roadside with the large showy orange blossoms of the day lilies and the smaller, more delicate purple blooms of the transplanted heather. The air smelled sweet and fresh, and Jamie recalled how enchanted she had been by the wild beauty of this region on her first trip. Today, however, in spite of the tranquil scenery surrounding her, she felt apprehensive. She made an attempt to recapture the peace this land had originally inspired within her, but was forced to admit defeat. The image of Josh was too strong.

As she drove into the valley where the park was located, her body tensed with the instinctive knowledge that he was present. Straightening and then arching her back to stretch the knotted muscles, she chided herself. What made her so sure he would be here? He hadn't come to the fashion show; he had chosen to remain in Europe with Selena. The thought of the blonde did not help her already jangled nerves. In a brief moment of honesty, she wondered what bothered her more—the thought that Josh was here or the thought that he was back in Pennsylvania with Selena.

Passing the building which housed the nature centre where visitors could learn about the fauna and wild life of the park, she crossed the high stone bridge below the dam and guided her car into the parking lot opposite the general store. It was nearly two o'clock and she hadn't eaten since breakfast. Answering the summons of her growling stomach, Jamie walked past the trout hatchery towards the dining lodge. There would be plenty of time later to check into the camping area and buy her tags and licence.

In spite of the brilliant October sun, a touch of winter in the air kept the day from being too warm. Hallowe'en was not far off and she was certain she smelled pumpkins. A smile found its way to her mouth, a smile which turned sour as she glanced around the dining room and her eyes were caught and held by the pale blonde hair of a tall slender woman sitting across a table from a dark-haired man. Turning abruptly, she fled. That Josh would bring Selena with him was a possibility she had not considered.

He hadn't seen her. She considered getting in her car

and leaving. She could call and have one of the Rangers tell him that she had car trouble and would not be able to make it to the park. But that was the coward's way out, and she had taken that route several times before where Josh was concerned. It had never worked. Besides, she was going to have to get used to seeing them together eventually. They were her neighbours. I'll move! The thought flashed through her mind, shaking her to the very core and arousing a depth of spirit she had not known she possessed. No one, not even Josh Langley, was going to chase her out of her home!

Changing direction, she marched up to the park office and registered for a campsite. At the store she bought some bread and milk and sandwich meat to lunch on while she set up her tent. The food tasted like cardboard and she gave up her attempt to eat after only a couple of bites. Even the physical exertion of pitching her tent and unloading her supplies did not help work off the tenseness in her. Tears continued to threaten, but her pride refused to allow them their freedom. She would shed no more tears over Josh Langley.

In an hopeless effort to erase the scene at the dining lodge from her mind, she wandered along the banks of the stream watching the fishermen, women and children, as well as the environment in general. In the fly-fishing area, beneath the shade cast by an old oak, a nest of tiny gnats was hatching on the surface of the water. The trout rose from the depths of their secure pool to feast on the delicacy with relish.

Returning to her campsite, Jamie set up her fly-tying kit and attempted to create a duplicate of the tiny insect. So intense was her concentration that she didn't hear the two men approaching until they were directly behind her.

'Now ain't you just the cutest thing ever to sit near a campfire!' A slightly slurred male voice broke the air above her.

Startled, Jamie turned to discover a large blond man

standing close behind her with a shorter, brown-haired man beside him.

'Don't pay him any mind, miss.' The smaller of the two men apologised, placing a hand on the fair man's arm and attempting to lead him away. 'He's had a little too much to drink.'

'Leave me alone—I know what I'm doing!' The larger man pulled free, refusing to follow his friend's lead.

'Come on, Larry, leave the lady alone.'

'How do you know she's a lady?' Larry's eyes glittered as they raked Jamie's body in a lurid manner.

'Larry!' His companion's tone expressed embarrassment.

'I didn't know drinking was allowed in the park,' Jamie remarked coolly, standing to face them.

'Wouldn't know about that,' the drunk responded, a silly intoxicated grin on his face. 'I did all my drinking on the way here, but we've got more in the car in case you'd like to join us for a little snort.'

'I don't think so,' she said evenly, attempting to humour the man. 'I'm really rather busy right now, so if you don't mind, I would appreciate it if you would leave.'

'Now ain't that sweet! She'd appre—appreci—like us to leave,' he mocked, swaying a little as he giggled and belched.

'Let's go, like the lady suggested,' his friend urged. 'I don't want any trouble.'

'Do you want any trouble, little lady?' Larry attempted to focus his glazed eyes on her as he spoke.

'I want you to leave.' In spite of the panic rising within her, Jamie was able to keep her voice calm.

'For a price,' he bargained. 'You've got a great body. How's about you and me taking a little trip into your tent!' As he spoke, he moved towards her, his heavy alcoholic breath causing her to feel nauseous.

'Larry, stop it! You're upsetting her,' his companion demanded angrily. 'You've said enough. Now let's go.'

'Just one little kiss,' the drunk persisted, capturing Jamie by the shoulders as his ugly mouth descended towards hers.

With her head turned in an attempt to avoid the man's unpleasant contact, she did not see the strong arm that wrapped itself around his neck, arching him backward in a painful position. With a cry of panic, he released her. 'Let go of me! You're strangling me! Dave, help me!' he pleaded, too intoxicated to mount a defence.

'You got yourself into this mess, you get yourself out of it.' Dave refused to come to his aid. 'Personally, I think he should beat you to a pulp—maybe that would knock some manners into you!'

'Okay, okay, I'll apologise. Lady, I'm sorry if I said anything to offend you.' Larry was frightened now. The silence of the stranger behind him produced an atmosphere of ominous danger. 'Lady, tell him to let me go,' he begged, placing his hope of rescue on Jamie. 'I didn't hurt you, did I?'

'Let him go—please,' Jamie requested in a quiet voice, near tears.

Releasing the man, Josh stood poised in case the drunk should decide to throw a punch in an effort to regain some dignity. But if there was any fight in the man it left him at the sight of those fierce black eyes levelled on him with murderous intent.

In cold silence, Josh watched as the man named Dave led his companion to a small sports car. It wasn't until the two men had driven off that he turned towards Jamie. 'Are you all right?' His voice was tightly controlled. 'Did he hurt you?'

'I'm fine,' she replied honestly, an embarrassed flush on her face. 'A little shaken, but fine.'

'Do you have to put up with mashers like that often?' His eyes were shuttered, but the vehemence in his voice frightened her.

'No. I've never had any trouble before,' she replied,

then in a more hesitant tone added, 'Thank you for your help.'

Josh didn't respond. Frowning darkly, he paced around the campsite taking in all of the details. 'Anyone could get into that tent at night.'

'You should know,' she snapped back, her nerves totally jarred by his intensity. The moment the words were out of her mouth she regretted the reminder of their first meeting.

There was an unreadable flash in his dark eyes before they again became shuttered. 'True,' he muttered, then in an authoritarian tone he added, 'Pack up. You're not staying here.'

'I am so,' she returned stubbornly. 'Those men won't be back.' He could wrap Selena around his little finger, but Jamie Kynter was not going to bow and scrape to his every whim!

'I don't intend to argue with you.' His eyes were chiselled charcoal as he began to gather up her equipment and load it into her car.

'Josh Langley, you stop that this minute! You're not my uncle nor my father, and you have no right to boss me around!'

'All right—you stay.' Josh set the tackle box he was carrying down on the ground. 'And I'll sleep here by the fire.'

'You can't—it's going to rain,' she choked out, startled by this solution.

'Then I'll have to share your tent.'

'I don't think Selena will like sleeping in such close quarters,' she shot back, digging her heels in and letting him know he couldn't make a fool of her again.

'You've really got Selena on your mind!'

'Are you going to deny it was her you were eating lunch with today? That you brought her along for . . . for . . . companionship?' Jamie faced him, her eyes green ice.

'She was an uninvited guest at my table—and no, I did

not bring her here for, as you so tastefully put it, companionship.' He met her gaze, his eyes hard and penetrating as if he could force her to accept his lies.

'I don't believe you. The day before I left Selena came to see me. She as good as told me that the two of you were getting back together.'

'The day before we were to have our talk?'

'The day before you were going to cajole me into this disgusting contest!' She wanted him to know she had seen through his little ploy.

'And you believed her.' It was a statement delivered in an introspective fashion as if it was the missing piece to a puzzle that had been bothering him by its absence.

'She was very sure of herself.'

'Selena's always very sure of herself. But in this case she has no reason to be.'

Jamie's eyes remained cold. The man used people, played games with their lives. She wanted to believe him, but she could not . They had been at war too long.

'You don't trust me, do you?'

'No,' she answered honestly. 'You came into my life in the middle of a storm, disrupted my peaceful existence, turned my world topsy-turvy—and I still don't know what you want of me.'

'Will we always be those two strangers who met in the night and parted so abruptly?' Josh questioned tightly.

'I don't know,' she confessed.

'There you are!' a familiar voice called out, startling Jamie, and she turned to face the new arrival. 'Got your note and walked over,' Joe Marley addressed Josh. Then turning his attention towards Jamie—said, 'This park is absolutely marvellous! You wouldn't believe the wildlife shots I've gotten over the last couple of days. And the lizards—I love them! Whenever one crosses over into another's territory they fight for possession. It's like photographing two tiny dinosaurs. Their size is perfect. The grass and leaves around them look like the ancient tropical forests.'

'I'm glad you're having such a good time,' Jamie forced a smile. 'But I'm surprised to see you here.'

'Didn't Josh tell you?' Joe looked more closely at the man and woman standing in front of him. 'I'd say I interrupted something. Shall I leave and come back later?'

'What is it Josh didn't tell me?' she demanded, ignoring his suggestion that he leave.

'That he's paying me an outrageous sum in addition to a week of cabin rental and meals to take a few pictures of you for the magazine. The "see Jamie Kynter at work" sort of stuff,' Joe elaborated in a subdued tone.

'You mean "see Jamie Kynter, Girl Fisherperson, doing her best in a contest staged by her too-zealous employer",' she corrected.

'Contest? Josh didn't mention any contest.'

'I decided against,' Josh announced nonchalantly.

Jamie stared at him in angry disbelief. 'Then why am I here?'

'It was on your itinerary?' he suggested, a coldly amused look in his eyes.

'Only because you were insisting on arranging that stupid competition,' she glared at him. 'Why didn't someone tell me you'd changed your mind?'

'And have Joe miss taking all those terrific pictures?'

'You tricked me!'

'And you walked out on our talk,' he reminded her as if that was vindication for his deception. 'You can't keep running for ever, Jamie.'

So he had manoeuvred her back to their beginning. But why? Suddenly, vividly, she recalled his statement made in the early morning dimness that they had left too much unfinished that night of the storm, and a knot tightened in her abdomen. He had made it clear that he wanted her, but there had never been any mention of love, and lust without love could never last. He would tire of her very soon after his conquest if she gave in to him. And it would be giving in on her part—he had made that abundantly clear too. He would not take her by force. He wanted her to come to him. Well, it would be a snowy day in July when that happened!

'Why do I feel like I've come in on the second act of a play?' Joe interjected, reminding Jamie and Josh of his presence.

'Because you have, but the first act wasn't any better than this, so forget it.' Josh's manner was curt as he picked up the tackle box he had set down earlier. 'I have to get Jamie packed up before it starts to rain. She's going to stay in my camper and I'll bunk with you in the cabin.'

Jamie started to protest, but bit back her words. Josh had won this round. He had correctly calculated that she wouldn't argue in front of Joe. If the photographer found out about the incident with the drunk he might mention it to her uncle, and she didn't want Howard to worry about her any more than he already did.

'Let me get a few shots first,' Joe requested unpacking his camera and checking the light.

'I feel like a hypocrite,' Jamie complained as she posed in front of the tent. 'I really think I should stay here.'

Josh shot her a warning look as he began to pull up the stakes securing the canvas, and she said no more. An hour later, her clothes moved into the camper, she found herself in the dining lodge with Josh and Joe as dinner companions.

'I couldn't help noticing that expensive camera outfit you have,' the waitress addressed Joe in a friendly manner. 'When I came in to work today, I saw you over by the hatchery. You do anything with your pictures?'

'Joe's a professional photographer,' Jamie explained.

'Are you his model? You're pretty enough for it,' the woman questioned.

'Personally, I think she's a bit on the skinny side,' commented Josh, rewarding the waitress with a wink.

Jamie's foot shot out, contacting his shin. His grimace

of pain gave her a malicious sense of pleasure. 'You're just impossible to please, Mr Langley. What's a poor girl to do?' she purred in a honeyed tone.

'Keep trying?' he suggested in a disturbingly provocative voice, making her wish she had kept her mouth shut.

The waitress gave Jamie a knowing look to say she understood how difficult a man could be, then addressing Joe again, returned the subject to photography. 'You should come in June one summer,' she suggested. 'You could get some great pictures during our Hillbilly Days. There's crafts, canoe races, greased pole climbing, square dancing and lots more. We even have a musket shooting contest between a Confederate team and a Union team. It's loud, but fun.'

'I'll consider it,' he promised, 'if you'll bring me a steak right now. I'm starved!'

Laughing goodnaturedly, the woman finished taking their orders and left.

In spite of Josh's presence, Jamie retained her appetite and when the food came, ate ravenously.

'I don't think Josh needs to worry about you staying too skinny for long,' Joe chuckled as they finished their desserts and sat drinking a last cup of coffee.

'I'm sure you'll work if off me tomorrow,' she returned, recalling their previous sessions. 'And while I'm thinking about it, I'd like copies of the pictures you took of me tying flies this afternoon.'

'All of them?'

'Yes. I thought I could use one of them for a cover.'

'Howard did mention that you were writing a book on fly-tying,' Josh commented. 'When it's ready for publication it would be a good idea to package it with a simple starter kit so that the readers can practise as they go along.'

'Every time I turn around the man is finding a new way to market me,' Jamie addressed Joe, her tone acid. 'I sometimes feel as if I should paste a price tag on my back!'

'But how would we ever determine what price?' Josh mused.

'It can't be all that bad.' Joe attempted to ease the tension beginning to build. 'Howard tells me your fan mail has increased dramatically.'

'True. I'm also getting categories of letters I never received before. In addition to the feminist mail congratulating me for making it in a man's world, I'm receiving obscene letters containing all manner of propositions, and then there are the marriage proposals, some with accompanying photographs and some without. I've been burning the obscene mail, but I'm keeping the marriage proposals in case Mr Langley decides to run a contest to see who gets me. You know, something like "Why I Want to Marry Jamie Kynter, in twenty-five words or less".'

'I would think three words would suffice,' Josh observed. There was a challenge in his eyes, daring her to ask him to say those words. She refused. She could not bear to hear him throwing the phrase around casually as if it were a joke. Forcing a yawn, she apologised and, pleading exhaustion, excused herself.

For the first hour after arriving back at the camper, she moved around restlessly, sitting first on the couch then at the table and finally in the upholstered passenger chair facing the huge windshield. Between bouts of chair hopping she paced, waiting for Josh's inevitable knock on the door. She was certain he would come. He had tricked her into showing up at the park and had arranged for Joe Marley to be there to take pictures, thus forcing her to remain overnight. He had even managed to manoeuvre her into the camper. For one brief moment the thought occurred to her that he might have arranged for the masher, but recalling the murderous look in his eyes she discarded that suspicion.

However, when he had not made an appearance after two hours she was forced to admit she had been mistaken. He was not coming. Allowing herself to relax, she gazed out the window of the camper. It hadn't rained as she had predicted. A brilliant full moon accompanied by the twinkling of millions of stars lit up the night sky like a pearl set in the mist of an array of diamonds. Unwillingly, Jamie found herself wondering how it would sound to hear Josh saying those three words in this moonlight under those stars.

His presence surrounded her, tantalising her, creating a longing she wanted desperately to deny but could not. She recalled the look on his face when he had asked her if they would always be those two strangers brought together for so short a time on that stormy night. Had she allowed that first traumatic encounter to shadow her reasoning? Had she kept him a stranger out of fear because of the hurt her instincts warned her he could cause her? If that was the case it had not been the solution. Even though he remained a stranger to her, she loved him.

Perhaps that was the way out. A ray of hope burned bright. Maybe she wasn't really in love with the man but only captivated by the mystique of the stranger. If she gave herself a chance to know him, maybe she could break this tenacious grasp he had on her. Tomorrow she would treat him not as an adversary but as a newly made aquaintance she wanted to know better. A danger signal flashed on in her brain, but she ignored it. 'I've got to settle this hold the man has over me once and for all,' she muttered aloud, determination sparking from her eyes.

CHAPTER NINE

Jamie had promised to cook breakfast for the two men the next morning. The bacon was frying and the coffee perking when their knock sounded on the door. Answering the summons, she was slightly disconcerted to find Josh standing there alone.

'Before you say anything,' he said, holding up his hand in a gesture of surrender, 'I want to apologise. I was wrong to trick you into returning here. I've asked Joe to take his pictures this morning so you can leave by early afternoon if you wish. I would like you to spend the afternoon with me, but I won't force the issue and I won't ask you to make a decision right this minute.'

'Apology accepted,' she responded in some confusion, surprised by this sudden change in attitude. She realised that she had counted on him remaining high-handed and arrogant, thus making it easier for her to convince herself that she really disliked him.

'And about breakfast,' Josh continued. 'Joe won't be joining us. He insisted on taking some early morning wildlife shots. So I thought I'd take you to the dining lodge to eat.'

'And waste all the food I've already prepared?' she questioned, determined to maintain her resolve of the night before. 'Unless you've decided you don't like my cooking.'

'Your cooking is fine.' He was watching her dubiously. 'Are you feeling all right this morning, Jamie?'

'I'm fine,' she assured him as she took up the bacon and started the eggs. 'How many eggs?' A smile played across her features. For the first time in their association, she had the upper hand. Josh was puzzled. She had

157

control of this game. A very dangerous game, a voice warned, but she paid no heed.

'Two, please,' He sat down at the table and watched her crack the eggs into the skillet. 'I have to admit, I expected you to accuse me of arranging Joe's absence.'

'Did you?'

'No.' His answer was firm and non-defensive.

Placing the eggs on the table, Jamie sat down across from her dark-eyed stranger. 'I hope everything is cooked the way you like.'

'Everything is just fine,' he acknowledged, regarding her curiously as they began to eat.

A stilted silence followed. Josh was leaving the direction they would follow up to her. 'I believe I read somewhere that you were from a large family,' she said.

'True. I'm the eldest of eight children, six boys and two girls.'

The mention of his sisters brought back vivid memories of his hands as they had expertly unbraided her wet pigtails. She swallowed hard. 'Tell me about them.'

He complied, beginning superficially until he determined that she was honestly interested. Then he allowed himself to speak freely about these people who meant so much to him. He spoke of his concern for their welfare and his pride in their accomplishments. His love for his family, shown openly and honestly.

'I would like to meet them some day,' Jamie heard herself admitting.

'That could be arranged. I know they'd like to meet you.' There was a warmth in his voice which penetrated to the depths of her soul, and she tensed. Things were not working out exactly as she had planned. Glancing at his watch, Josh let out a low whistle. 'Joe's going to think we've deserted him!'

'My equipment is still in the car,' she recalled as she headed for the door like a bullet. 'Where do we start?'

'On the bridge.'

Intuitively, she knew he meant the bridge on which she had sat the first time she had seen him.

'I thought you two had forgotten me,' Joe greeted them. 'It's a good thing I had this tree to keep me occupied!'

Josh looked questioning at the man as if he was losing his mind, while Jamie laughed and directed her employer's attention to the sparsely leafed branches above him. They were decorated with various lengths of fishing lines from which dangled an odd assortment of lures like ornaments on a Christmas tree.

'I think I've got a great cover picture,' the photographer quipped. 'We can call it "The Fishing Tree".'

The laughter following this remark was of a companionable nature, setting the tone for the rest of the morning. For the next few hours, Joe snapped pictures of Jamie in various activities related to fishing as well as fishing itself at different locations throughout the park. Josh remained with them, carrying equipment and helping when he could but keeping any suggestions he might have to himself and letting Joe direct the proceedings. Once, during a break, Jamie had glanced over at him questioningly.

'And you thought I was impossible to get along with!' he tossed back at her as if he could read her mind. When she blushed, indicating that he had correctly guessed her thoughts, he smiled openly and she had returned the smile. It was a warm, shared moment that stayed with her.

As they finished lunch, Joe announced that he intended to spend the afternoon photographing nature and suggested that Jamie and Josh catch dinner. 'I've been here three days and haven't tasted a trout yet,' he noted bluntly.

'Joe is in for a disappointment,' Josh commented as the older man walked away.

'Disappointment?' Jamie questioned.

'Unless you've decided to stay a while longer, I don't

believe he's going to have that trout. I've done a little ocean fishing, but that's about it.'

'Are you telling me you've never fished for trout? That all that expensive equipment in your camper is strictly for show?' she chided goodnaturedly.

'Nor catfish, bass, carp or bluegill, to name a few others.'

'There has to be something sacrilegious about the owner of a hunting and fishing magazine knowing so very little about one of the sports,' she bantered.

'Both. Knows little about both,' he corrected. 'I don't even own a gun.'

'Goodness!' she declared in mock alarm. 'That leaves me no choice but to stay and teach you how to fish for trout. If your lack of experience should ever become public knowledge no one at the magazine would be able to hold their heads up again!'

'I must remember to write my father and thank him.'

'Thank him?'

'For preferring golf to fishing,' he elaborated with a heart-stopping smile.

'I'll check your equipment and get it ready ready while you run over to the store and buy your tags and licence.' Jamie cleared her throat nervously as she rose and began stuffing the paper cups and plates from the impromptu picnic they had just shared into a trash bag. Their fingers accidentally touched as they both reached for the same cup, and it was as if an electric charge had swept over her body. Jerking away, she dropped the container. 'I'm so clumsy,' she muttered selfconsciously.

'Not nearly as clumsy as I have been,' Josh returned in a quiet cryptic tone. Then pushing himself swiftly to his feet he was on his way to the store to purchase the necessary documents.

As Jamie put together one of the rods and reels from the stock of equipment in the camper, her hands shook slightly. The hold Josh had over her wasn't an infatuation with the mystique of a stranger. It was a deep, abiding love. And what was truly wonderful was that she was beginning to accept the possibility that he might actually care for her. He had said Selena had lied and she wanted to believe him.

They spent the afternoon laughing together at times and being peacefully silent at others, but always contented with one another's company. Josh was a fast learner, and that coupled with beginner's luck produced a fish by the end of their first hour on the river.

'I have my dinner,' he announced. 'Now it's up to you to catch yours and Joe's. You're the expert.'

'And what do you plan to do for the rest of the afternoon,' Jamie questioned.

'Watch you. I love watching you.'

Jamie blushed and promptly hooked her line in a tree.

He jokingly chided her, making wisecracks about helpless women as he pulled the branch towards the ground to retrieve her line. 'You mustn't be upset,' he remarked in a solicitous manner for the benefit of a passing fisherman. 'I've heard that even the experts have trouble getting their lines out once in a while.'

The man gave Josh a knowing look. 'Try to get her to understand that it's all in the wrist. She doesn't have to throw her whole arm.'

Josh's eyes danced with merriment.

'You're impossible!' Jamie told him in a strangled whisper as she fought to control the laughter bubbling inside.

'Now, remember, it's all in the wrist,' he said very loudly as he handed her back her line.

'Maybe I should hook his hat,' she threatened, eyeing the helpful fisherman maliciously.

Josh caught her arm before she could cast. 'But then he might feel compelled to take over your lessons, and I don't want to share you with anyone.'

A warm glow spread through Jamie and she averted her eyes so that he could not read the depth of emotion his words had evoked.

Towards evening they found themselves back on the bridge where they had begun their day. As they sat quietly, their lines resting in the water, a question that had been nagging at the back of her mind demanded to be asked. 'Josh,' she began cautiously, not wanting to destroy the peace between them, 'I have to admit that I'm a little curious. Why is Joe . . .'

'In a cabin instead of sharing my camper?' he completed the question when she hesitated.

'Yes.'

'Not because I was planning to lure you into my private haven and seduce you, although that's not a bad idea,' he answered non-defensively. 'He's in a cabin because the only way I could get him to come was to promise him accommodation for a week and I didn't know how long I would be staying.'

Jamie flushed slightly at his ability to read her thoughts.

'As long as we're being perfectly candid with one another,' he continued, 'why don't you tell me what Selena told you that set you against me?'

'I already told you she insinuated that the two of you were going to get married again,' she hedged, too unsure of herself to brave mentioning the woman's other accusations.

'That's not what I'm talking about. I want to know what she said to you that night she called for the interview. She said something that's bred a strong thread of distrust of me into you.'

Unable to face him, she stared out over the water. 'She mentioned your Pygmalion complex.'

'My what!'

'Pygmalion complex,' she repeated, her voice barely above a whisper.

'I heard you the first time. And you believed her?'

'You were demanding some very drastic alterations in my life.'

'True. But I wasn't doing it for any personal pleasure.

Can you belive that?' There was an urgency in his tone.

'I want to.' She bit her lip as she glanced towards him.

Reaching out, Josh brushed a wayward strand of hair from her face. 'It was clear to me that you wanted the magazine saved. Bringing you out into the open to generate publicity was the best plan I could come up with.'

'I understand.' She wanted desperately to believe him.

'And I confess, maybe I did want to bring you out of that Never-Never-Land you were living in and make you grow up a little.'

'You wanted me to become more liberated.' Her voice was stiff.

'No, not liberated in the sense you're obviously considering. Less naïve is more what I had in mind. Ever since that night we met, I haven't been able to stop worrying about you when you're out on one of your camping trips.'

Looking closely at him, Jamie noticed for the first time that he too had lost some weight and had tiny tired lines near his eyes. 'You don't need to worry about me. I learned my lesson,' she told him.

'Like the masher yesterday?' The anxiety in his voice was mirrored in his eyes. 'If I had my way I'd lock you up in a tower away from the rest of the world and only I would have the key.'

'That's a very chauvinistic attitude,' she stammered.

'I feel very chauvinistic where you're concerned.' There was a rawness in his tone that thrilled her. 'I won't lie to you, Jamie. I want you. But I won't force you into anything you aren't ready for. I'm willing to wait.' He stroked her face with the back of his hand. 'For a while,' he qualified.

Reaching up, she captured his hand and carried it to her lips. She felt his body tense as she kissed the strong tanned skin. 'I do need some time,' she said, her lips moving against the warm flesh.

'Only a little while,' he returned, emphasising the 'little,' as he leaned towards her and brushed her lips with his mouth.

Over his shoulder she noticed a couple of fishermen watching and quickly pulled away. 'We're attracting attention.'

Straightening away from her, he laughed. 'I do enjoy seeing you blush. Maybe I should kiss you more soundly and see what kind of a crowd we would draw.'

'Josh!' she said his name warningly, although inwardly the thought of being in his arms produced a warm expectant glow within her.

'Later, then.' It was a promise.

Over dinner with Joe, they joked and laughed. For the photographer's entertainment, Jamie recounted Josh's successes and failures, ending with the proclamation that the man had a natural talent and with practice could become legendary. Josh, in an effort to maintain his end of the conversation, suggested that Joe take a picture of Jamie with her line in a tree to give the average fisherman a boost in morale.

Soon after the meal was finished, Joe announced that he was tired and was going back to the cabin.

'Do you think he guessed we wanted to be alone?' Josh asked with an amused gleam in his eye following the man's departure.

'He's very observant, and luckily for you,' she bantered, 'not too protective.'

'He knows I'd never do anything to harm you.' There was a softness in his voice that warmed her. 'And now I'm going to take you for a walk in the moonlight.'

As they strolled along the riverbank, a mildly chilling breeze caused her to shiver. Releasing her hand, Josh wrapped his arm around her. They didn't speak, yet Jamie felt as if so much was being said. She sensed a closeness to this man she knew she would never experience with anyone else.

She shivered again and coming to a halt, he drew her

against his long length. 'I've been very patient, but now I intend to fulfil my promise from the bridge.'

She made no protest when his mouth claimed hers. Trembling, she strained against him, her hands burying themselves in his thick black hair.

As her lips parted under his passionate assault, she was filled with a burning longing so strong her knees weakened, forcing her to cling to him for support. Their bodies seemed to melt together in the heat of the embrace and the world around them vanished as she allowed her hunger for him to guide her response.

'You make waiting very difficult,' he murmured against her skin as he explored the hollow of her neck.

'And you frighten me,' she admitted, her instincts suddenly warning her to pull back.

'Is it me or your emotions?' he whispered harshly, nibbling on her earlobe and making thinking difficult.

'I'm not sure.' The words came out hesitantly, her insecurity dampening her ardour.

Josh sensed her withdrawal. 'And I promised you some time to understand yourself better,' he sighed, releasing her. 'But only a little while.'

Cupping his face in her hands, Jamie drew him towards her to place a light kiss on his lips. 'Thank you.'

'But only a little while,' he reminded her with a gentle laugh, his eyes caressing her possessively.

'Only a little while,' she agreed, her fears dissolving, to be replaced by the belief that he honestly did care for her.

Back at the camper, he drew her into his arms, claiming a last tender kiss before opening the door and letting her go in. 'Thank you for a wonderful day,' he said, looking up at her as she stood silhouetted in the doorway.

'You're more than welcome.'

'Breakfast tomorrow?'

'Breakfast tomorrow.'

As if he could not bear to be so close to her and not test

the softness of her skin, he reached out and ran his fingers along the line of her jaw. 'Goodnight, Jamie Kynter. Sleep well, and dream of me.'

'I will.' It was a promise that would be easy to keep. The temptation to ask him in was strong, but a warning voice cautioned her to go slowly. 'Goodnight, Josh.'

Closing the door, she sat down on the cushioned couch and gazing out at the moon, held on to the feeling of his presence. She loved him with a depth she had never thought was possible, and she was beginning to believe that he returned that love.

A sharp knocking startled her out of her reverie. It came a second time, louder and harder. Had Josh come back? The thought filled her with trepidation and excitement both at the same time. She wasn't certain if she could send him away again, and she would never be able to trust him if he took advantage of her weakness towards him after he had promised to give her time to understand herself and her emotions.

As she opened the door, her softly questioning expression hardened into anger as Selena pushed past her and into the camper. 'I saw that cute little display a few minutes ago. I would think a proper little girl like yourself would be ashamed to have allowed herself to be kissed by a man who's already spoken for!'

'He's not engaged to you.' Jamie responded curtly.

'Is that what he told you?' Selena's voice was honey-coated contempt. 'What a little fool you are! I thought you had more brains than that.'

'Will you please leave?' Jamie held the door open, glaring at the blonde, who moved around the camper nonchalantly picking up an item here and there, examining it and then laying it back down.

'When I'm ready,' Selena replied in a lazy drawl, a half smile tilting one side of her mouth. 'Cosy—very cosy!'

'Get out!'

'We really must have one of our little chats first. I

so enjoy them.' Selena seated herself on the couch Jamie had so recently occupied. 'Tell me, would you have?'

'Would I have what?'

'Would you have let Josh stay if it had been him at the door?'

'That's none of your business.' Jamie's voice was liquid ice.

'It's my guess that you wouldn't have,' Selena purred. 'Breaking down a spinster's defences takes a little longer.'

'I'm not a spinster!'

'I'm sorry if I offended you, dear. I thought that was what unmarried virgins your age were called, and you're so very obviously one of those women who believes in saving herself for marriage.'

'Get out!' Jamie demanded again, feeling like a broken record.

'Of course, that first passionate love can dull one's sense of reason,' Selena continued undaunted. 'And where Josh is concerned, a woman doesn't have a chance. He's so very much a man. I've never been able to forget our life together.' She sighed wistfully, a sensual smile curling her lips.

'You seemed to be able to forget him long enough to remarry,' Jamie snapped, a hard knot forming in her stomach.

'There are some opportunities a woman simply can't resist,' Selena mused, a cynical gleam in her eye. 'However, my second marriage is totally irrelevant to our conversation.'

'This conversation is irrelevant. We have nothing to talk about.'

'You mustn't be so hasty. And you're wrong, very wrong. We have a great deal to discuss. I do so want to save you from any unnecessary pain.' The blonde's pitying eyes fell on Jamie much as a mother might look upon a wayward daughter.

'I can take care of myself!' Jamie's eyes flashed angrily.

'My dear, don't you see that Josh is only interested in you because you're a challenge? That man can't resist a challenge, especially a virgin. You're quite a prize.'

'I'm neither your dear nor a prize!' Jamie hissed back, feeling shaky in spite of her resolve not to listen to this woman.

'Now, now, you mustn't get yourself upset. I'm only trying to help.' Selena took a cigarette case out of her purse and looked around as if searching for something. 'I see Josh has given up smoking—unless you've hidden the ashtrays. I know you outdoor types don't approve of us smokers.'

'I haven't hidden anything.'

'Of course not. How silly of me! You're such an innocent. If he was still smoking you would probably be lighting his cigarettes for him. I can even picture you bringing him his slippers in the evening and sitting on the floor next to his chair while he reads the paper.' Selena paused for a moment to shake her head sympathetically. 'You'll never do, you know. You'll bore him to death within a week. Perhaps even one night is all he'll need.'

'If you have such a low opinion of me, why waste your time coming here to talk?' asked Jamie coldly.

'Because I'll confess, you've become so much of a challenge to Josh that he might marry you to bed you. I'm not interested in waiting for him to realise his mistake and then go through a long divorce proceeding before we can be together again where we belong.'

'I'm sure if you belonged together, he wouldn't be interested in me.' Jamie's voice held a conviction she did not feel.

'You don't know the man. I was married to him—I understand his drives, his needs.' Rising from the couch, Selena moved towards the door. 'Just keep in mind, Miss Kynter, that Josh loved me and with a man like him an emotion like that runs deep. I admit we had our problems and I'm as much to blame as he. We were both very involved in our careers. However, I now realise that he was the most important thing that ever happened in my life. I intend to have him back, no matter how long it takes.'

Jamie watched the woman leave, her body braced against the door for support. She didn't want to believe Selena, but so much of what the woman said made sense. Josh had referred to their first meeting as unfinished and she herself had accused him of seeking her out to appease his male vanity. Also, although he had made it very clear that he wanted her, he had not mentioned love or marriage. But most disconcerting was the fact that he had been married to Selena. This was something she could not overlook. She knew the man well enough to know he would not marry on a whim.

First she cried. Then she lay swollen-eyed, staring at the ceiling, forcing herself to face reality. She loved him too intensely to be used and then discarded. Bitter tears dripped on to the pillow as she reached a decision. She would ask him about his marriage to Selena. His refusal in the past to discuss the woman had left her with an underlying fear that he still harboured strong feelings towards her. It was better to face this truth now than to find out later that she had been a fool.

She dozed for an hour or so, waking with the sun. Splashing cold water on her face, she dressed quickly. Then, opening her suitcase, she threw the few articles necessary to complete her packing into the leather bag and snapped it shut.

She made coffee but didn't cook any breakfast. The thought of food nauseated her. Josh arrived as she was taking her first swallow of the black liquid. It felt like acid on her stomach.

'I confess, I told Joe to eat elsewhere this morning,' he said with a warm smile, then glancing around the camper, asked, 'Are we eating elsewhere, too? Or am I early?'

'I'm late,' she apologised tightly.

He approached her, a concerned look on his face. 'You don't look too good. Are you sick?'

'I'm fine. I just had a bad night.'

'You don't look or sound fine.' He placed his hand on her forehead to test her temperature.

'I'm okay,' Jamie insisted, knocking the hand away.

'Well, something's wrong. Are you going to tell me what it is, or do we spend the morning playing Twenty Questions?' He was treating her like a child and she sensed a deep underlying anger in him.

'Selena paid me a visit last night after you left.'

'Selena?' His voice was like ice. 'What did she want?'

'She wants you.' The statement was delivered in a vacant, resigned tone.

'She can't have me.'

'She's still in love with you.' Jamie studied her coffee cup, unable to face him.

'Selena never loved anyone in her life except herself.'

'You married her.' The words came out barely above a whisper. He had not denied loving the woman.

'My marriage to Selena is not a subject open to discussion.' There was black finality in his voice.

Jamie fought back the tears. The woman must have seriously wounded him to have left so great a scar, and she could only have done that if he had loved her deeply.

'What did Selena say to you exactly?' he questioned.

'It doesn't matter,' she replied hollowly, pushing her coffee cup aside and rising. 'I have to be leaving. My uncle will be expecting me.'

'You can call him and tell him you've been delayed.'

'No. I really have to be on my way.' Her voice was quiet, yet determined. She turned her face away, unable to endure his blazing stare.

'It all boils down to a matter of trust, doesn't it?' Josh's voice was bitter. 'Either you trust me or you don't.'

'I suppose so,' she admitted, her head throbbing so badly she could hardly speak.

'Don't run away from me this time, Jamie.' The harshly delivered statement was a plea, a threat, a warning all at the same time.

'I need time to think.'

'I would say you spent the night thinking, and I lost.' His tone was cynical and there was a cruel twist to his mouth. 'You'd rather trust someone like Selena than me.'

'I don't even trust myself where you're concerned!' she choked out as she picked up her suitcase.

Josh made no physical move to stop her, but as she neared the door his voice sliced across the heavy stillness between them. 'If you turn away from me this time, I won't seek you out again.'

For a moment she hesitated then Selena' mocking image flashed into her mind. Knowing she loved him too much to always be second in his heart, she pulled open the door and walked out into the bitter sunlight.

CHAPTER TEN

Jamie was never certain how she managed to drive home. She drove past exhaustion, stopping only for a few hours at a time to curl up on the front seat and sleep. Each time it was a fitful, dream-filled sleep, and always the same dream. She was lost in a deep dark cavern and Selena's voice kept telling her over and over again to give up, there was no way out. Jamie called to Josh for help, but he didn't answer. Even awake he haunted her. His last words, the finality of the statement, repeated itself again and again in her brain. 'I'll survive. Somehow, I'll survive,' she told herself, but the core of her very being felt as if it had died.

When she arrived home, Howard sent her directly to bed and called Dr Evans. The man came, examined her, made some vague pronouncement about a lot of viruses going around and left. For four days, she slept and at various intervals ate a little at Howard's urging. Finally, with the dawning of the fifth day, she opened her eyes, looked at the sunshine pouring in her window and decided it was time to face the world once again.

'I'm glad to see you're feeling better,' Howard greeted her as she joined him on the patio. He insisted on helping her with her chair and fussed over her, wanting to know what he could fix her for breakfast.

Jamie felt guilty for having put him through the worry he had experienced on her account these past few days. 'I'll just have some orange juice and coffee right now, but I promise I'll eat an egg and toast in a little while.'

'I want you to take it easy today. Don't overdo. You've been pretty sick.'

'I promise on one condition,' she bargained.

'And what's that?' he smiled, glad to have the old Jamie back.

'That you go in to the office today. I know you've stayed here with me these past few days and must be champing at the bit to get back to your desk.'

'I don't like the idea of leaving you alone.'

'I insist. I feel fine.'

'I'll only go in if you'll swear that you'll take it easy and rest.'

'Cross my heart,' Jamie promised, adding bitterly to herself, 'what there is left of it'.

On his way out, Howard returned to the patio to check on his niece one final time. 'By the way,' he said, 'if you feel up to it, you should call Maggie. I ran into her at the grocery store the other day and mentioned that you were ill. She's been calling every day since to ask about you. In fact, that soup you had the other day came from her kitchen.'

'I'll think about it,' Jamie replied unenthusiastically. She liked Maggie, but the woman's close association with Josh made having her for a friend out of the question.

Howard kissed her goodbye and, after reminding her of her promise to take it easy, departed.

She sat for a time staring down towards the wooded area housing the stream which created a barrier between her property and Josh Langley's. Had her pride been worth what she had given up? But then it hadn't been pride. Not really. It had been a matter of survival. He would have left her eventually for Selena, and after having been with him, sharing his bed, experiencing him totally, she knew his desertion would have destroyed her. Brushing a loose strand of hair back from her face, she noted sarcastically that she wasn't doing too terrifically as it was.

This truth shook her, bringing a frown to her face. Pushing herself out of her chair, she went up to her room and dressed. Then she made herself two soft-boiled eggs and some toast. Surprisingly, the food felt good on her stomach. Going back out to the patio, she stretched out in a chaise-longue, covering herself with a light blanket. In the soft morning sun, she rested, dozing off and on. It was as she was waking from one of these short naps that she sensed she was not alone.

'I hope I didn't startle you,' said Maggie, putting down her knitting and smiling warmly.

'Have you been here long?' Jamie covered a yawn with her hand.

'Only a short while. I had my knitting to keep me company. I'm so pleased to see you're feeling better.' Maggie peered closely at the younger woman as if to assure herself of Jamie's recovery. 'You still look a bit drawn. I hope you plan to take it easy for the next few days.'

'You sound just like Uncle Howard!' Jamie accused as she stretched and sat up.

'Now don't you go getting up on my account.'

'I need something to drink.' Jamie moved towards the house. 'Can I get you some iced tea, or would you prefer something hot?'

'Iced tea will do fine.'

Returning shortly with the drinks, Jamie chose to sit in one of the chairs closer to the older woman. 'I hope the tea suits you. I didn't add any sweetener.'

'Lovely, just the way I like it,' Maggie assured her, taking a second healthy swallow before setting the glass aside and resuming her knitting.

'What are you making?' Jamie asked, watching the woman's hands move deftly.

'It's a layette set for my newest grandchild.' Maggie beamed proudly as she pulled out the already finished sweater and booties in a variegated green yarn. 'All I have left to do is the blanket.'

'They're lovely. I'm sure your grandchild will look adorable in them.'

'I had hoped to be knitting a layette set for a child of Joshua's one of these days soon.'

'You probably will,' said Jamie, forcing herself to face the unpleasant truth. 'Selena's determined to have another go at marriage with him.'

'Selena?' Maggie's voice was filled with contempt. 'She may want to have another go at it, but I'm certain Joshua won't want to have anything to do with that woman.'

'He married her once,' Jamie persisted, the words causing a tight knot in her stomach as she voiced the thought that had been running through her mind like a broken record for the past several days. 'He must have felt deeply for her once, and a man like Josh wouldn't be able to dismiss those feeling entirely.'

'No. If Joshua loved a woman he would always love that woman,' Maggie confirmed. 'But love was never a factor in that marriage.'

'I don't understand.'

'It's rather a sordid story.' The housekeeper hesitated momentarily, as if experiencing an inner struggle, then reaching a decision, continued. 'I thought maybe Joshua would have told you the story, but on the other hand, I guess he wouldn't. It's not exactly the kind of experience one likes to recount. In fact, other than him and Selena, I believe I'm the only other person who knows the truth.'

'What is the truth?' Jamie coaxed unashamedly, her nerves taut with the need to know.

'They met at a party,' Maggie began. 'Selena was twenty-seven or eight at the time and still a junior editor on the magazine where she worked. Joshua was twenty-two and already on his way up in the publishing world. He used to go to lots of wild parties in those days. He doesn't any more. I guess his experience with Selena washed the taste for such things out of him.' Maggie paused as she changed directions in her knitting, being careful not to drop a stitch. Outwardly, Jamie waited patiently, while inwardly she wanted to scream at the woman to continue.

After what seemed like an eternity, Maggie picked up the narrative. 'The first time I saw Selena was when she showed up at our door early one morning and demanded to see Joshua. She told me later that they'd had a torrid affair, but I'm certain it was nothing more than a one-night stand. Joshua didn't even recognise her name when I told him she wanted to see him that morning. Anyway, they went into the study and talked, and when she left there was a "cat who ate the canary" look on her face. Joshua called me in and told me he was getting married and that I should fix up the spare bedroom as a nursery.

'It seems that Selena had told him she was pregnant and sworn that the child was his. Joshua has too strong a family instinct to turn his back on his own offspring, so he married her. He didn't treat her badly either. She had an insatiable appetite for expensive clothes and jewellery and he bought them for her. I guess he did it mostly because he felt guilty for neglecting her. They hadn't been married more than a month before he started working later and later at the office. Sometimes he wouldn't come home at all. I couldn't blame him. Selena was a difficult woman when she didn't get her way. I know, she made my life pretty unpleasant.

'Then Joshua had to leave town on business. The very afternoon he left, she told me she wasn't feeling well and was going to see her doctor. When she came back, she refused to eat any dinner and went to bed early. Knowing how upset Joshua would be if anything happened to the baby, I fussed over her. I checked on her several times during the night and she appeared to be sleeping just fine. You can imagine my shock when she came into the kitchen the next morning saying that she'd called her doctor and was on her way to the hospital. I immediately grabbed my coat and purse, but she refused to let me accompany her. She said I'd never been kind to her and that the possibility of losing the baby was upsetting enough without having to put up with someone who hated her. I was really hurt. I admit I didn't like her, but I'd gone out of my way to treat her with the respect she deserved as Joshua's wife. I was never unkind to her.'

'I'm sure you weren't,' Jamie offered consolingly as Maggie paused, obviously expecting a response.

'No, I wasn't—and that wasn't all. She said I wasn't to tell Joshua that she was in hospital if he called and I wasn't to call him. She said she knew his business was more important to him than her or the child and that she didn't want him to be bothered. I assured her she was wrong and he would want to know, but she insisted, and threatened me with dismissal if I disobeyed her.

'She came home from the hospital the day before he was due home, all teary-eyed. She said she'd had a miscarriage and that I was to tell Joshua when he got home, because she was too upset to face him. That was the hardest thing I've ever had to do. He blamed himself for leaving her when she needed him.

'She made me give away all the nursery things I'd bought—claimed they upset her—and then she moved into the spare bedroom. She and Joshua hardly spoke to one another. Selena decided she wanted to go back to work and insisted that since she'd quit her job to have his baby, he should find her a better position than the one she left. He had enough pull to find her a very good job and he did. He gave her a few months to get back on her feet and then suggested that they call an end to the farce of a marriage they were living, but she refused. She said he was trying to make a laughing stock out of her by marrying and divorcing her in less than a year. She took to taunting him about the miscarriage, too—blaming him for the loss of the child.

'She's a cruel woman, and that was her undoing. She taunted him once too often and he paid a visit to the doctor. It took some doing, but he found out the truth.' Maggie put down her knitting and looked Jamie directly in the face. 'She hadn't had a miscarriage at all. She'd had an abortion.'

Jamie's heart cried out for the pain Josh must have felt on learning this.

'I'll never forget the night he faced her with that bit of information. I've never seen him so angry. I think he could have killed her with his bare hands. Selena was frightened, too, but she still tried to place the blame on him. She claimed she'd done it because she knew he hated her and would hate any child she bore him. Only this time Josh didn't buy her lies. He threw her out. He told me to pack all of her things in boxes and set them in the hall. He said she was never to be allowed to cross his threshold again. But even then she still got herself a sizable divorce settlement. She gambled that Joshua wouldn't want the publicity that would have surrounded a messy divorce action and she was right. Once she was out of his house he simply wanted her out of his life for ever and was willing to pay the price.'

'I can't believe she would kill Josh's child,' said Jamie, her voice catching with emotion.

'I'll tell you what I told Joshua.' Maggie leaned towards the dark-haired girl in a conspiratorial manner. 'I told him that I believed she had the abortion because she wasn't sure what the baby was going to look like. I don't think she honestly knew who the real father was.'

'What did he say to that?'

'He didn't say anything. I think he'd already considered that possibility himself.'

'You said that only you, Josh and Selena know this story. Why tell me?' asked Jamie.

'Maybe I shouldn't have, but I know how much Joshua cares about you and I've been afraid that Selena might try to cause trouble. She hates him and would still like to get even with him for throwing her out the way he did.'

A deep pain filled Jamie. She had played right into Selena's hands by listening to the woman's lies and fearing her own emotions. She had lost Josh, and she had no one to blame but herself. She had not followed her heart. She had not trusted the man she loved.

'I wouldn't want anything that witch might concoct to come between the two of you,' Maggie continued, returning to her knitting. 'I can't tell you how happy I was when Josh handed me those two pictures of you and told me to buy the nicest frame I could find, because he loved that girl in those photographs and intended to marry her.'

A moan escaped from Jamie.

'Are you in pain, dear?' Maggie was at once solicitous. Putting down her knitting, she hurried over to place a hand on Jamie's forehead to see if her temperature had returned. 'You do look pale. I'm afraid I've stayed too long. I only meant to stay a moment to be certain you were all right. I wanted to be able to assure Joshua when he calls—if he calls. I really don't understand that man. I haven't heard from him since he was left for Bennett Spring except for a telegram saying he was going to stay away a while longer than he'd previously planned. I guess he decided he needed a vacation, and I can't blame him. I can't remember the last time he took a few days off just to relax. But I know that if he'd known you were ill he would have come home immediately.'

'I am feeling somewhat tired,' Jamie interjected into this long-running dialogue, hoping that the woman would leave before the tears that burned at the back of her eyes poured over.

'Yes, you do have small circles under your eyes. Now, you just lie back down where I found you and have another little nap.' As she spoke, the housekeeper led Jamie back to the chaise-longue.

'Thank you, I will.' Jamie promised.

'And I'll be on my way.' Maggie stuffed her knitting into a canvas carry all. At the corner to the house she turned back to wave. 'I'll call again later in the week to see how you're getting along.'

Jamie waved weakly, her strength going to hold back the tears of agony which began to overflow the moment Maggie was out of sight. She had allowed her insecurities to destroy everything. Josh had said he would not seek her out again and she knew from the look in his eyes that he had meant it.

Her uncle mentioned Josh that evening too. 'Heard from Josh today,' he said as they sat down to eat dinner. 'He called to tell me I was doing a great job with the new format and he planned to leave me alone for a while. Said he hadn't taken a vacation in years and thought he'd go out West.'

Jamie's appetite vanished. Josh couldn't even stand to be in the same state with her.

Joe Marley came by during the middle of the next week to show Jamie the photographs he had taken of her at Bennett Spring. On his way out he handed her a manila envelope, explaining that he had taken a few candid shots she might like to have.

After he left she opened the envelope to find several photographs of herself and Josh sitting on the bridge late in the afternoon. The unguarded expression on his face told her how much she had given up when she had walked away from him. 'It can't end this way,' she muttered aloud, determination flashing in her eyes. With that thought a tiny spark of hope began to grow. He had said he wouldn't come to her but that didn't mean she couldn't go to him.

Over the next couple of weeks, she debated with herself about the best way to approach him. She could simply face him and tell him how much she loved him and beg him to take her back. But there was always the chance that Maggie had exaggerated his feelings for her and he might laugh in her face or her distrust of him might have killed any love he felt towards her. He had never actually mentioned love or marriage to her and her instincts for survival warned her that facing his rejection would be devastating. However, she refused to give up without a fight. He had faced her rejection not once but several times. She owed them both this one last chance.

For hours on end she paced around the house talking to herself, practicing various versions of the same speech. Her nerves was taut. She could not rid herself of the fear that he would not want her. Not now. Not after she had shown so little faith in him. Not after she had listened to Selena's lies.

Selena. When Jamie thought of that woman now she saw things so differently. The interview for instance. Somewhere in the back of her mind she had always suspected that Josh had shown up that day to see Selena. Now she knew that he had come only to protect her, Jamie Kynter, fool extraordinaire. He had forced himself to associate with a woman he despised for her sake and she had treated him like an interloper.

It was on a particularly pleasant fall day that Howard entered the living room carrying the mail to find his niece sitting on the couch staring into space, her mind deeply preoccupied. He had noticed her tenseness the past few weeks, but when he tried to talk to her about what was bothering her, she had been evasive. 'Here,' he said, tossing her a large yellow envelope with lots of red scrawlings across the front. 'Win yourself a camper like Josh Langley's.'

The mention of the person who was occupying her every thought brought Jamie out of her intense reverie. Absently she picked up the piece of junk mail and opened it. Several particles of paper fell out. There was a page giving information on the contest rules while another large folded sheet contained pictures and descriptions of all the prizes being offered in this particular sweepstakes drawing. Also included was the entry blank with a request to return it promptly and another brightly printed page informing her of the extra bonuses she could receive if she was one of the winners and had returned the entry blank by a certain date. Stuffing the material back into the oversized envelope, she tore it in half and dropped the pieces into the wastepaper basket.

Sinking back on the cushions of the couch, she recalled the dinner in the dining lodge at Bennett Spring when she had chided Josh about making her the prize in a contest. Suddenly a small seed of an idea began to grow.

The next morning she was up early working at her desk. After several unsuccessful starts, many revisions, some deletions and a few tears, she wound a fresh sheet of paper into her machine and typed:

WIN A BRIDE!

Jamie Kynter, writer of the Duckbill's Daughter column for *Meadow and Brook*, in deciding to change the scope of her column to a more family orientated fishing and camping guide has found that she lacks certain elements to add authenticity to her work—A HUSBAND AND CHILDREN.

Miss Kynter is considered by those who have sampled her culinary skills to be a passable cook, although not a gourmet.

She is relatively well educated and reads other material besides hunting and fishing guides, thus being enabled to converse on several subjects in an intelligent manner if not in depth.

She can, in most cases, speak and write in complete sentences and spell most words with the aid of a dictionary. She has some trouble with crossword puzzles and needs a great deal of help with the larger versions found in the Sunday paper.

She is kind to small animals and children and can bake chocolate chip cookies.

She is reasonably attractive and has been told that at times her eyes are exceptional.

Miss Kynter does, however, possess a few minor faults. She has a temper and a tendency to be unsure of herself. Her greatest fault, one that she is determined to overcome, is that in the past she has not followed her heart. She was afraid of being hurt and in an attempt to prevent irreparable damage to herself did run away from a man she desperately loved. She quickly learned that running away physically could not break the emotional ties she felt towards this man and the damage occurred anyway. If you are interested in helping her repair her broken heart and following through with her plans for adding credence to her writing and if you meet the following requirements, fill in the blank on the back of this page stating in twenty-five words or less 'Why I Would Like to Marry Jamie Kynter'.

Requirements: Contestant must be thirty-four years of age, dark-haired and dark-eyed. He should like the outdoors and must love children. He does not have to know a great deal about fishing. His name must be Josh Langley.

Pulling the sheet of paper out of her typewriter, Jamie turned it over and drew in an entry blank. She then re-read what she had written several times. It wasn't perfect, but it would have to do. As she folded it carefully and placed it in an envelope, she admitted to herself that she was taking the coward's way out. If Josh did not want her, he could throw the paper away and she would not have to face his rejection in a physical confrontation.

Slipping the envelope into her bag, she walked across her back lawn, over the small bridge spanning the stream, climbed the stile over the fence, and then crossed Josh's lawn to his house. Maggie was pleased to see her. She had several pictures of her newest grandchild she wanted to show Jamie. They sat chatting for quite a while before Jamie worked up the courage to ask about Josh.

'I'm expecting him any day now,' the housekeeper

told her, then added in a concerned tone, 'You two had a quarrel did you.'

Jamie nodded in the affirmative.

'Don't you worry. You'll kiss and make up.' Maggie spoke with a confidence Jamie wished she felt.

'Actually that's why I'm here today. I have a favour to ask of you.' Before she could change her mind, Jamie reached into her bag and pulled out the envelope with Josh's name on it. 'I was wondering if you could see that he gets this when he returns.'

'This quarrel between you and Josh was serious, wasn't it?'

'Yes, and it was my fault. But I'm hoping to undo the damage I've caused to both him and myself.'

'I'm sure everything will work out just fine. The two of you are so right for each other.' Maggie took the envelope and gave Jamie a reassuring hug.

That evening Howard remarked about how nervous she was and suggested that she go to a movie to get out of the house, but Jamie pleaded a headache. She didn't want to chance being gone if Josh did return and call.

The next day was even worse. She started four different novels, but not one of them could hold her interest. She baked a double batch of cookies and a cake. 'If Josh doesn't get home soon, he won't be able to chide me about being too skinny,' she muttered aloud to the empty kitchen. However, when she cut herself a piece of the cake, she found she had no appetite. Later in the afternoon she strolled down to the stream, but even there she could not relax.

'Josh is back. Had lunch with him today.' The words uttered so nonchalantly by her uncle on his return home that evening had the effect of a physical blow.

'Did he say anything about me?'

'Just asked how you were. You don't have to worry—I don't think he has any new plans for you in the immediate future.'

Howard was standing with his back towards her,

pouring himself a drink as he spoke. Before he could turn and see the pain etched in her features, she fled. Locking herself in her bedroom, she stood with her arms wrapped tightly around herself, trembling, too damaged to cry. Dizziness began to overcome her. Realising that she had been holding her breath, she gasped for air. Unconsciously rocking back and forth she tried to regain some equilibrium as dry hacking sobs issued disjointedly from her throat. The phone rang, but she ignored it.

A couple of minutes later Howard knocked on her door. 'Jamie, Maggie's on the phone. She wants to talk to you.' When she did not open the door nor respond, he demanded, 'Jamie, can you hear me?'

'Yes, I can hear you. I was just going to take a shower,' she lied, attempting to keep her voice level. 'Tell her I'll talk to her tomorrow.'

She heard his footsteps retreating and collapsed into a chair as a slow steady stream of tears flowed down her cheeks.

The footsteps returned. 'She says it's important,' Howard relayed the message through the door. 'Maybe you should talk to her.'

'All right,' she agreed with a sigh as she picked up the extension next to her bed. Although she was in no mood to listen to Maggie's consoling words telling her that everything would work out in time, she did not want to have to explain to her uncle about what was going on.

'I thought I should call and warn you. Josh got home a few minutes ago. Actually he's been in town most of the day, but he stopped by the magazine before coming home. Anyway, I gave him the envelope and after he read the contents he took off for your place at a healthy clip. He was walking pretty fast, so I imagine he'll be there real soon.' There was laughter in her voice. 'I told you everything would be just fine.'

'Thank you for calling. Thank you so much,' Jamie managed to choke out before she hung up. Wiping the tears from her face. She checked her hair. She considered changing, but her hands were shaking too badly.

'What did Maggie want that was so important?' Howard asked as she hurried out on to the patio.

'Josh is on his way over,' she answered, her attention riveted on the line of trees, watching for the first glimpse of him as he emerged.

'I wonder what he wants. I hope it's not another contest,' he remarked from behind his evening paper.

'I hope it is,' she responded, causing him to look at her dubiously.

Josh hadn't appeared and she began to feel uneasy. Unable to bear the waiting any longer, she started down towards the stream.

Howard Kynter watched his niece depart with a shake of his head. 'The problem with little girls is that they grow up into irrational impetuous women,' he muttered with a fatherly grin as he returned his attention to his paper.

It wasn't until Jamie was crossing the footbridge that she spotted Josh. Her legs weakened and her breath caught in her lungs. She was like a person who had been lost in the desert without water and had suddenly stumbled upon a mountain spring as she stood drinking in the sight of him and knowing that she would never get her fill.

He was sitting on top of the stile, a pen in one hand and her typewritten sheet in the other. Looking up, he saw her. 'I thought I'd better write my answer down. I don't want to be disqualified on a technicality.' His tone was deadly serious, his manner intense.

Hesitantly, she moved towards him. Slipping his pen back into his shirt pocket, he stepped down from his wooden perch and stood waiting for her. Her hands shook as she accepted the paper from him and turned it over to read what he had written.

'I want to marry Jamie Kynter because I love her more than life itself and without her I am not complete.

P.S. I think four children is a nice number but will settle for two.

Josh Langley.'

'Oh, Josh,' she stammered, her voice choked with emotion, 'I do love you so very much!' Tears glistened in her eyes as she moved into the circle of his arms. 'I was so afraid you wouldn't want me any longer.'

'You're an integral part of me, Jamie. I couldn't stop wanting you even if I tried,' he murmured gruffly as their lips met in a long hungry kiss.

When she trembled from the sheer joy of feeling him close to her, he drew a sharp breath and his hold tightened pressing her firmly against his long length.

His body was taut and she sensed his need to be reassured that this time she would not run away from him. Moving her hands over his back in strong caressing motions, she deserted his mouth to place tiny kisses over his face and into the hollow of his neck. And with each kiss she murmured words of endearment and promises that she was his totally and completely.

As his body relaxed, she met his lips for a second long tender encounter before breaking the contact to gaze up into his strong featured face.

'Does this mean that I win?' he questioned huskily, a smile playing at the corners of his mouth.

'No, it means that I win,' Jamie replied, looking lovingly into his soft mink eyes.

'We both win,' he corrected with a pleased laugh, before recapturing her willing mouth for a renewed assault.

When their lips parted several minutes later she straightened away from him slightly. 'Josh, there's something I have to tell you,' she said, her voice holding a nervous tremor.

'Tell me you love me, Jamie,' he commanded.

'I love you,' she returned, letting him read the truth in her eyes.

'Then that's all I want to know.'

'Josh, please!' Her voice held a plea. She wanted everything in the open between them.

'All right. What is it?' he frowned, unconsciously tightening his hold on her as if he was afraid she might slip away from him again.

'I know about Selena—Maggie told me. Please try to understand. It was important to me to know. I loved you too much to be second in your life. When you refused to talk about her, I assumed you still loved her. I couldn't bear the thought of having you and then losing you.'

Relief flooded his features. 'I do understand. I should have told you myself. After you left I had a lot of time to think, and I realised that if you'd been married before I would have had doubts. I know I hated the thought of you ever having been with another man. That day I questioned you about your on-the-road-encounters, for instance. I knew I was being crude, but I couldn't help myself. I had to know—not for the magazine but for myself.'

'Yourself?' Her tone was incredulous. 'But you were so hostile towards me!'

'Hostile, frustrated and confused,' he admitted with a shake of his head. 'I hadn't been able to get you out of my mind since you ran from my camper the night of the storm. Awake or asleep your image haunted me, taunting me with those lovely tigress eyes. In fact, for a moment when I walked into Howard's office and found you there, I thought I was hallucinating.'

'I know the feeling,' Jamie confessed, placing a light kiss on his lips before adding in a slightly accusatory tone, 'You scared me half to death that morning, both in my uncle's office and during the drive home.'

'I know, and believe me, I've paid dearly.' The pain mirrored in his eyes told her of the depth of his anguish. 'When I followed you into the kitchen and found you crying, I hated myself, and I knew then that I was hopelessly in love with you.'

'You knew then?' Jamie choked.

'Yes, I knew then. I stood there watching you, knowing how much I'd hurt you and not knowing how to make amends or if you would even let me try. Then you came into my arms and allowed me to comfort you, and it gave me hope that I could undo the damage I'd done. Though there were times when I almost lost that hope . . . and then when I thought you'd finally forgiven me, you turned away from me again.' A shudder shook him as he sought her lips once again to assure himself of his victory.

Jamie's fingers wound into his hair as she raised up on tiptoes and added her own strength to the kiss. 'I'd forgiven you long ago,' she breathed against his lips. 'It was only my stupidity in listening to Selena's lies that was keeping us apart. I'm so sorry. I was such a fool.'

'Oh, Jamie!' Josh crushed her to him until she could hardly catch her breath. 'Every time you were in the same room with me, you were a threat to my sanity. I had to force myself to treat you with kid gloves.'

'The "kid" gloves was part of the problem,' she frowned. 'I thought you saw me as a child.'

'So that was why Selena was able to sell you on that Pygmalion idea so easily,' he groaned.

'That and my own lack of faith in myself as a woman,' she admitted, as he released his hold until she was standing loosely in the circle of his arms, her hands resting on his shoulders.

A gleam sparked in his eyes. 'Now that's something I'm going to enjoy proving to you.'

'Proving what?' she questioned in a mild state of confusion.

'Just how much of a woman you really are,' he elaborated, his eyes darkening to expose the fathomless depths of the desire she awoke in him.

An excitement unlike anything she had ever known

swept through Jamie. Her hands slid beneath the collar of his shirt, circling the strong cords of his neck. 'You're . . .' she hesitated, searching for the right words to tell him how much he meant to her.

'Impossible?' Josh suggested with a crooked grin.

'Impossible,' she agreed, her jade eyes dancing as she raised up on tiptoe to run her lips along the line of his jaw. 'Marvellously impossible!'

ANNE MATHER

Anne Mather, one of Harlequin's leading
romance authors, has published more
than 100 million copies worldwide,
including **Wild Concerto**,
a *New York Times* best-seller.

Catherine Loring was an
innocent in a South
American country beset by
civil war. Doctor Armand
Alvares was arrogant
yet compassionate.
They could not ignore
the flame of love igniting
within them...whatever
the cost.

HIDDEN IN
THE FLAME

Available at your favorite bookstore in June, or send your name, address and zip or
postal code, along with a check or money order for $4.25 (includes 75¢ for postage and
handling) payable to Worldwide Library Reader Service to:

Worldwide Library Reader Service

In the U.S.
Box 52040
Phoenix, AZ
85072-2040

In Canada
5170 Yonge Street, P.O. Box 2800,
Postal Station A
Willowdale, Ont. M2N 6J3

HIF-A-I

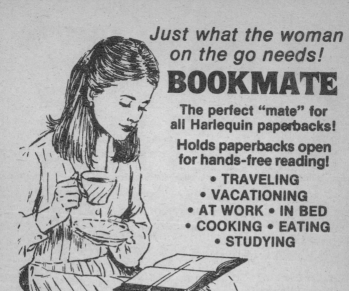

Just what the woman on the go needs!

BOOKMATE

The perfect "mate" for all Harlequin paperbacks!

Holds paperbacks open for hands-free reading!

- TRAVELING
- VACATIONING
- AT WORK • IN BED
- COOKING • EATING
- STUDYING

Perfect size for all standard paperbacks, this wonderful invention makes reading a pure pleasure! Ingenious design holds paperback books OPEN and FLAT so even wind can't ruffle pages—leaves your hands free to do other things. Reinforced, wipe-clean vinyl-covered holder flexes to let you turn pages without undoing the strap...supports paperbacks so well, they have the strength of hardcovers!

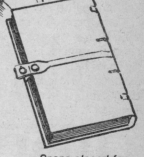

Snaps closed for easy carrying.

Available now. Send your name, address, and zip or postal code, along with a check or money order for just $4.99 + .75¢ for postage & handling (for a total of $5.74) payable to Harlequin Reader Service to:

Harlequin Reader Service

In the U.S.A.
2504 West Southern Ave.
Tempe, AZ 85282

In Canada
P.O. Box 2800, Postal Station A
5170 Yonge Street,
Willowdale, Ont. M2N 5T5

MATE-1R